Risking It All For My Hustla

Chyna L.

(Based on true events)

Text Grandpenz to 22828 to stay up to date with new releases, sneak peeks, contest, and more...

Check your spam if you don't receive an email thanking you for signing up.

Text SPROMANCE to 22828 to stay up to date on new releases, plus get information on contest, sneak peeks, and more!

2020

<u>Prologue</u>

"Aaliyah! I'm home! I took an early flight back from my book signing. Nana said you weren't feeling good. What's wrong with you, girl?"

"OH SHIT!" I jumped up from under my comfy covers at the sound of my mother's nearing voice. I looked over to my right and looked at my alarm clock. It was 7:00 AM. She wasn't supposed to be back in town until noon. I looked over to my left and my boyfriend, Dwayne, was still sound asleep, snoring with drool trickling out the side of his mouth. I shook his arm roughly.

"Wake up! Dwayne, wake up! Wake the fuck up! My mother is here!" I started panicking as I heard her high heels clicking up the stairs towards my room. I was cornered with no escape. Dwayne finally got up out of my bed, yawning and stretching without a care in the world.

"Damn yo', I was knocked." I put my hand over his mouth.

"Shut up, bae! My mother's home early! Go in here and be quiet!" I pushed him into my closet right before my mother swung my door open.

"Oh, hey, Ma," I said nervously, fidgeting with my too small pajama shorts.

"Hey, Yaya I thought you weren't feeling good. Why aren't you in bed?"

"Oh, I'm... I'm not. I was just about to go get some... some juice." I could kill myself for stuttering; it was a dead giveaway.

"Juice? Really? That's interesting because I already see a cup of juice on your nightstand. Two, actually. So, you must be realllll thirsty." I hung my head low. Busted.

"Yeah, that's what I thought. Where is he?" There was no point in trying to lie my way out, so I simply pointed to my closet. My mother opened the door and Dwayne walked out, head hanging low just like me. I watched as she escorted him to collect his stuff and then out of my room without saying another word. I sat on the edge of my bed, waiting for whatever was about to come next. Five minutes later, she walked back into my room.

"Why do you have that nappy headed ass little boy in my house, Aaliyah?" Before I could answer, she started speaking again.

"How many times do I have to tell you that you're not missing out on anything by focusing on school and only school? These little knuckleheads out here don't have nothing to offer you. Not even the one I just kicked out."

"But I love him!" I blurted out without even thinking.

"You love him?" I shook my head yes. She took in a deep breath and then sighed.

"I knew this day would come, Aaliyah, so to be honest, I ain't even mad at you. But what I need you to know is this; everything you think you're doing or think you're gonna do, I've already done it, baby girl." She threw a black book on my bed and walked away. I rolled my eyes. *What the fuck am I supposed to do with this?* I picked it up and looked at the cover. No title, no author. Now, I was curious.

I flipped to the first page and started to read.

2003

Chapter 1

I sat on the bench, bouncing my leg up and down, trying my hardest not to bite my acrylics. I hated to see females with chewed up fingernails. It made them look manly and raggedy. I looked to my right and my home girl, Christina, looked just as nervous as me. Shit, I think I even saw sweat on her forehead and it damn sure wasn't hot in here. Truth be told, we both had every right to be nervous. Here we were, fourteen years old, skipping school, in a courthouse two towns over from where we went to school. All so my fast ass could get permission from a judge to get an abortion without my mother knowing about it.

I don't even know how I got myself into this fucked up ass situation. This shit wasn't supposed to be happening to me. Not like this. I was what most people would call a "good girl". I went to a private school, got good grades, and never got into any trouble. I had a smart-ass mouth, but what girl my age didn't? Even still, I was my mother's only child and she put me up on a pedestal every chance she got to anyone who would listen. I hated when she bragged about me, but it never stopped her from doing it.

But unfortunately, being a single mother in the hood of Boston was hard, and that forced her to work overnights as a nurse to make ends meet. She asked my deadbeat father to step in and spend more time with me so that he could keep an eye on me while she worked. He said he would, but he never actually did. I ended up home alone almost every night. That's where the trouble began. At least three nights out the week, I would sneak my boyfriend, Donte over to chill while my mother was at work. My mother didn't even think I paid attention to boys, so she never suspected that I had a boyfriend. Donte and I had been kicking it for a few months now. He wasn't even my first boyfriend. Actually, he was my third, but he was the first boy that I had sex with, one time, and we used a condom, so this shit made no sense to me. Yet, here I was.

****

"Didn't I tell your dumb ass I don't like onions on my shit?!" Troy threw the burger onto the sidewalk. *I looked at him and then looked at the burger on the cement. I had spent my last two dollars on that burger and he just threw it on the ground like it was nothing. I sucked my teeth.*

"You do know I could've just taken the onions off for you, right? You didn't have to waste my money like that. Mad fucking rude." Before I could suck my teeth again, he roughly snatched me up by my arm and twisted it behind my back in one swift motion.

" Yo', who the fuck you think you talking to, V?" he said between clenched teeth with a frown on his face that I had never seen before. When he first grabbed me, I thought he was playing, but the serious look on his face told me that he wasn't. Or maybe he was. I tried my luck.

"I'm talking to you, nigga! Now get your hands off me!" I tried pulling away. He twisted my arm harder. I grimaced in pain. Now I knew for sure that he wasn't playing.

"No the fuck you are not. I will break your arm right fucking here if you even think you talking to me like that. You got it?" I wanted to say something smart back so badly, but the persistent pain in my arm told me that he might just break my arm right here in broad daylight, in front of all these people, so instead, I gave in.

"Yeah, I got it." He let go of my arm and smiled.

"Good. Now let's go. I'ma show you how you supposed to order my burger next time since you fucked it up this time." He walked off towards the Burger King entrance. I examined my arm where he had grabbed it and noticed that it was already beginning to bruise. I shook my head, knowing that I had to get myself out of this so-called relationship. And after a few more domestic disputes with Troy, I did. But now...

"Victoria Morris."

The judge calling my name snapped me out of my horrible memories of my first boyfriend, Troy. Although he had never pressured me into sex, he was very abusive physically and verbally. At first, it was just verbally. But when it started to get physical, I knew I had to let him go; especially because my mother never even knew he existed in the first place. I was proud that I managed to get myself out of that situation safely and with my virginity still. But, with that being said, I was even more disappointed in myself at this very moment for being right back in a bad situation. I wiped the sweat off the palms of my hands and entered the judge's chambers with my head down.

****

"So, how'd it go? They gonna let you do it? Or you gotta tell your mother? That was mad fast. That can't be a good thing. What happened, V?" Chrissy asked all in one breath.

"Damn Chrissy, chill. They said yes. I just gotta wait for the consent papers in the mail to bring with me to my appointment." I looked over at the clock on the wall. "It's still early; if we hurry up, we can make it to school by third period."

"Orrrrr we can head to the Galleria and chill there for the day." She was such a bad influence.

****

Later on that night, I called Donte to let him know that I got the okay from the judge. This nigga had the nerve to say "Thank God" and then tell me he was going to call me back. I mean, I couldn't expect him to say much more, but him brushing me off like that did hurt my feelings a little bit. I sat patiently for an hour, waiting by my house phone for him to call me back. I had so many mixed emotions about what I was about to do and I honestly just needed someone to vent to. Plus, I wanted to know how he felt about the situation. He hadn't said much since I told him. All he wanted to know was when my appointment was. After two hours of watching the phone and bursting into tears randomly, but repeatedly, my eyes started to get heavy. I don't know why I thought crying and watching the phone would help, but the phone still hadn't rang. To be honest, I didn't even know why I was crying. I had been an emotional hot mess ever since I found out I was pregnant and I hated it. Eventually, I just said fuck it and took my emotional, pregnant ass to sleep. I reminded myself that my appointment was in two weeks and then this whole nightmare would finally be over. I got myself into this situation, so now I had to get myself out of it.

****

Six Weeks Later

It had been a month since I got rid of my baby and I was just now starting to feel like myself again. Donte wasn't checking for me like he used to so when he asked to come chill for a few hours while my mother was working, I jumped at the opportunity. I missed what we used to have. As soon as we hung up the phone, I showered and threw on my cutest Hello Kitty pajama set, glossed up my lips, sprayed on my sweet pea body spray and waited for him to get to my house. Although he lived on the other side of town, he usually rode his bike over, so I knew he would be arriving in no time. I was excited to be spending some quality time with my boo; I couldn't even sit still and wait. Instead, I paced back and forth, checking the window every few minutes just in case I didn't hear the doorbell.

An hour later, he showed up with his cousin, which was fine with me. They kicked it on my couch, watching football while I cleaned the kitchen like my mother told me to do before she left for work. I washed the dishes and eavesdropped on their conversation at the same time.

"Yo', Dee, what day was that last week that we went downtown?" his cousin asked.

"Nigga, everyday! You know niggas stay going downtown after school," Donte responded.

"Yeah, I know, but I'm talking about the day you copped your new shorty them Jordans."

New shorty? New sneakers? I knew good and well that I hadn't gotten shit from Donte but some dick and a baby, and I damn sure wasn't new, so what new shorty and sneakers? I instantly saw red. I charged into the living room, soapy butcher knife still in my hand.

"YOU DID WHAT?!" I got directly up in Donte's face. My adrenaline was pumping and my attitude was on "I don't give a fuck".

" Yo', chill with that fucking knife in your hand! You bugging!" I could see the nervousness all over his face, but at that moment, I didn't give a shit. I was ready to stab his ass up. It wasn't even about the sneakers; it was the principle. This nigga had me out here looking all types of stupid, clearly.

"I'm bugging? No, nigga, YOU bugging! I've been sitting at home in pain and sad for weeks because I killed OUR baby and you running around buying the next bitch sneakers! And don't you dare lie and say you didn't because I heard everything!" I followed up with a mush to his big ass forehead. He jumped up off the couch and grabbed my arm.

"Don't you ever put your fucking hands on me, girl! You crazy? Yeah, I did buy another chick some kicks. So? Get the fuck over it and get the fuck up out my face with all that rah-rah shit. Ayo, JoJo, let's go! We out!" He pushed past me and headed for the door while I sat there, butcher knife still in my hand, crying my eyes out.

"Donte, wait!" I yelled after him. "Who is she?" I wanted to know what was so special about this bitch that she was getting gifts, when lately, I had to beg just to get his attention. I guess I knew why now. I couldn't help but wonder where this mysterious chick even came from. Was it someone that I knew? Was it someone at his school? I had a million and one unanswered questions running through my head.

"Who is who? Man, listen; I ain't even tryna talk to you right now, to be honest. Especially while you still got that big ass knife in your hand. Maybe I'll call you later or something, but right now, I ain't tryna hear it." He walked out the door without even giving me a chance to respond. I sat there in the middle of my hallway floor, crying my eyes out, rocking back and forth. I just couldn't understand what this was that I was feeling right now or why it was even happening. I stared at the door, waiting for Donte to walk back in and pick me up from the floor. I was waiting for him to come take the now dry butcher knife out of my hand, hold me close and tell me he was sorry and that she didn't matter;

whoever she was. I sat there, in that one spot, for hours, and I waited. But, he never came back.

That night, I called his phone over one hundred times and left at least twenty voicemails, begging him to at least talk to me. He never answered or responded. The next morning, I went to the spot in Ruggles T station where we met every school morning, hoping he would be there. He wasn't. I waited twenty minutes, not caring that I would be late for school. He never showed up. Eventually, I had to accept the fact that it was over and at fourteen years old, I was already experiencing the first of many heartbreaks to come.

2004

Chapter 2

I can't front, the breakup with Donte had me stressing for a few months. Shit, he was my "first love". To ease the pain, I kept my head in my books and stayed focused on school. I could tell that my mother was starting to notice a change in my attitude and I wondered if she could tell that I was fucking. Even if she did know, I damn sure wasn't going to say anything if she didn't say anything. Don't ask don't tell was my policy when it came to her.

"What's with the attitude lately, Victoria? Every time I say one damn word to you, you start jumping down my throat. It's beginning to piss me off." It was too early in the morning for this. My mother never chilled and she wondered why I always had an attitude.

"I don't know what you talking about. I don't have no attitude," I said with an attitude.

"Yeah, okay. Just get your ass up and get ready for school," she responded, walking out of my room.

"Whatever," I mumbled under my breath. She quickly turned back around.

"You got something to say?" I knew better.

"Nah."

"Oh, okay. That's what I thought."

I couldn't wait until I got the fuck up out of this house with her. I don't know what her beef was with me, but it was ruining my life. All I was trying to do was live like all the other girls my age. I guess that was too much to ask for.

****

It was Friday, and since all my homework was done, my mother let me go spend the weekend with one of my favorite older cousins, Mimi. That's when I met Drew.

Drew was two years my senior, the star basketball player at his high school, and one of the ugliest, cockiest niggas you'd ever meet. The night I met him, he told me I was going to be his girl. I laughed in his face. He smiled with his chipped tooth and damn near demanded that I allow him to take me to the movies the following weekend. I knew I had nothing else better to do, so I agreed. My social life had been nonexistent since my break up with Donte, so I figured getting out would be good for me. I had to give it to Drew because as ugly as he was, he was a smooth ass nigga. Call me a sucker, but by the end of our movie date, I was wearing his chain and had agreed to be his girl just like he said I would.

Being Drew's girl became my life. He was "that nigga" and being on his arm had my young ass feeling like I was "that bitch". He showed me off to everyone, never caring that I was younger than he was. Only a few weeks into our relationship, we were already having sex, and even though he wasn't my first, he was definitely showing me the ropes.

Drew was bringing out the inner freak in me that I didn't even know existed. At only fourteen, I was ready and willing to learn it all and he had no problem teaching me.

"You gotta make sure you got enough spit in your mouth so you can get it nice and wet. Don't try to be all pretty with it. Get sloppy, boo," he told me when giving me lessons on how to suck his dick the right way. I had never even considered sucking dick until now. My friends would die if they knew, but I didn't care. For Drew, I would do anything.

"Start off slow and steady and then increase your pace, but not too fast, aight? You don't wanna make a nigga bust before you get yours. But this is your time to shine, so give it all you got while you up there," Drew told me while teaching me how to ride his dick to perfection.

When he was hitting it from the back, he would slap my ass and yell, "Throw that ass back, baby." I loved that shit. To say Drew had me dick-whipped was an understatement. I started coming home later and later after school just so I could fuck him for hours before his mother or brother got home. Of course, me coming home late caused mad tension between me and my mother, but I didn't care; Drew was all I needed.

****

It was my fifteenth birthday and my mother agreed to take me to Canobie Lake Theme Park for the day. After days and days of begging, she also agreed to let Drew come along. I was too amped to have my boo by my side for the day. I put on my cutest pum-pum shorts I could find to give him something to look at while we walked around the park all day. My mother brought one of her girlfriends along for the trip so that she would have someone to keep her company and eventually, that worked in my favor. She wasn't paying me and Drew half as much attention as she would've been if she was by herself.

"Ma, me and Drew gonna go over there and play games so he can win me something, OK?" I caught her in mid-conversation, that way, she would brush me off like she always did. After getting the hand wave that meant OK, Drew and I headed over to where all the games were, but on the way, I stopped.

"Oh, look! A photo booth! Let's take pictures, boo!" I pulled at his arm like the little girl that I was. He laughed at me.

"I don't know about no pictures, but I got another idea of what we can do in there." He had a sly grin on his face and I had a confused look on mine.

"What you mean?" He grabbed my hand and pulled me towards the picture booth. As usual I followed his lead, ready and willing to do whatever.

"Just come on before somebody else goes in. I'ma show you what I mean once we get in there."

I stepped inside the small booth and he stepped in after me, closing the curtain behind him. The space was so tight it could barely fit the two of us. I watched as he sat down on the small bench where people usually sat to take their pictures. He turned me around so that my back was facing him and I was standing between his legs.

"Drop them little ass short to your ankles." My eyes grew super wide as I snapped my head around to look at him in disbelief.

"Say what?" He smiled.

"You heard what I said. Pull them shorts down and come sit on this dick real quick and then I'ma win you the biggest stuffed animal out there." He was so convincing. I turned back around and did as I was told. I bounced up and down on his dick until we both were satisfied. I couldn't believe what I had just done but it did feel good. Afterward, Drew won me the biggest stuffed animal I ever owned, just like he promised he would.

****

Drew and I were madly in love with each other. Or at least that's the way it seemed…until I got pregnant…AGAIN. The night I told Drew I was pregnant , he looked me in my face and said… absolutely nothing.

"Damn Drew, say something. Please!" I begged with tears welling up in my eyes. I couldn't understand how I had let this shit happen again. I had to be the stupidest chick alive.

"What you want me to say, Victoria? Listen, I love you and all that good shit, but next year I graduate and I'm tryna get a scholarship to play college ball out of state. I ain't about to let nothing or no one fuck that up for me, yo'. So, honestly, I don't know what to tell you, ma. Parenting ain't in my short term or long term goals right now." He looked away into the night air. I looked at the side of his face, waiting for him to say more, but he didn't.

"Well, what happens if I decide I want to keep it?" I already knew I wasn't, but I just needed to know that if I did decide to go that route, he would support me.

" I'ma tell you like this. If you decide to keep that baby, V, you gonna be on your own." I felt my heart crush. I really thought that what Drew and I had was real. He had always supported me when it came to school or when I was beefing with my mother. But now it was like he was saying "fuck me" and that shit hurt me to my core.

"Okay, Drew. Say no more," was all I could bring myself to say as I walked away towards the bus stop, tears flowing from my chinky eyes, down my caramel-colored face.

It took me two weeks to get up the courage to tell my mother. When I finally did, she was more hurt than she was mad, but she stood by my side like she always had. She took me to the clinic a week later to abort yet another baby. This was my second abortion in less than two years and my body wasn't feeling that. I laid on my couch, thinking this must be what death feels like. The pain I was experiencing was almost unbearable. I got up to go to the bathroom and check to see if I had bled through my pamper-like pad again, but before I could make it there, I got lightheaded, then dizzy, and then everything went black…

Chapter 3

I woke up in a hospital bed with my mother sitting beside me, holding my hand.

"Ma, what happened?" I asked hoarsely. The last thing I could remember was lying on the couch in pain, wondering where the hell Drew was since he hadn't even bothered to check on me after my procedure. Even still, it didn't look like his ass was anywhere to be found. Before my mother could answer, a young, white nurse entered the room.

"Hi, Victoria, how are you feeling?" she asked kindly.

"I'm okay, I guess. Just in a lot of pain still, but what happened? Why am I here?" I asked with a confused expression.

"Well, after your procedure today, you started to hemorrhage. You lost a significant amount of blood and that is what caused you to lose consciousness. I have to be honest with you; if the ambulance did not arrive as quickly as it did, you might have died." I stared at her in disbelief at what she had just said.

"Miss Morris, have you ever had any previous abortions before today?" she continued. I swallowed hard and looked over at my mother, who was staring at me with a blank expression, waiting for my response.

"No, ma'am," I whispered.

"Hmm, that's interesting," she responded, flipping through my charts on her clipboard. I shuffled in my bed. I felt like a hooker in church. I said a silent prayer that this nosey bitch didn't keep prying in front of my mother. I was in pain and in no mood to confess to my first slip up. The way my mother was set up, she would kill me right in this hospital bed.

"Well, I'll be right back with your discharge papers. No heavy lifting of any kind, no sexual intercourse, and no alcohol for at least the next week or two. Try to stay off your feet for the next few days as well if you can. I will also be giving you a prescription for pain medication." I silently said a good looking out prayer to God for helping me dodge that bullet.

"You okay?" my mother asked me as soon as the nurse left the room.

"Yeah, I guess. But where's Drew? Why ain't he here? Did you tell him what happened to me?" It was one thing for Drew to not go with me to my appointment, but the fact that I had just damn near died and he still wasn't around was dead wrong. *His ass better have a great excuse for not being here right now,* I thought.

"Drew knows that you're here. I called his mother as soon as we got you stable and settled. She said she would let him know where you were and tell him to call my phone immediately. I haven't heard from either of them since. But don't worry yourself about Drew. He's a man and sometimes men can be very insensitive to critical situations. That's why you need to be more careful of the situations you get yourself into, Victoria. Take this as a lesson and always remember it's Momma's baby but Daddy's maybe." She couldn't have been more right.

****

Over the next few days, I stayed in bed mostly. Drew's bitch ass came by to check on me one time and all he did the entire time was watch basketball. I mean it wasn't like there was much that we could do, given my current physical condition, but I damn sure didn't expect to stare at the back of his head the entire visit.

"Damn Drew, you ain't even looked my way once since you've been here," I said, sucking my teeth and rolling my eyes.

"Why would I need to? You ain't doing shit but laying there. We chilling. Just be happy I'm here 'cause I could be home playing my game right now," he said nonchalantly, without even looking away from the TV.

"And just exactly what is that supposed to mean? Are you tryna say that's where you'd rather be?" I didn't know what the hell his problem was, but I wasn't going to force him to keep me company or be at my house if he didn't want to. I didn't need anyone doing me any favors.

"No, what I'm tryna say is stop complaining for once. And can you turn the TV up? I can't hear." All I could do was shake my head in disbelief at how inconsiderate and insensitive he was being towards someone that he claimed to love so much.

"You can't hear because we're talking, duh. But I guess you wouldn't know that 'cause it ain't like we talk much anyway unless it's about sex or sports. Feel free to correct me if I'm wrong, please." No response. I sucked my teeth and rolled over to take a nap. Talking to Drew while he was watching a game was like talking to a brick wall, pointless. He reached under my pillow, grabbed the remote, and turned the TV up anyway. *Asshole.*

****

After I was fully healed, I went right back to school and got my mind in place to take my tenth grade MCAS exams. Drew and I had started speaking less and less since the abortion. I was so busy catching up in school that I barely noticed until one night while sitting on my bed, painting my toenails, it dawned on me that I hadn't seen or heard from Drew in three days. I called his cell phone and after two rings, a female voice answered.

"Hello, who's this?" she asked.

"Ummm, what you mean who's this? Read the name on the screen, honey," I said with much attitude. Drew had my number saved under "Wifey" from the day we started dating, so I knew this bitch knew who I was.

She chuckled. "Actually, *honey*," she mocked me, "there is no name saved to this number. So again, who is this?"

I sucked my teeth. "Look, boo, I don't know who you are or why you're answering MY man's phone right now, but you need to put Drew on the phone before shit gets ugly." This bitch had me fucked up if she thought she was just going to sit on the other end of the phone and clown me like I was a sucker. I wasn't a fighter, but I damn sure wasn't a sucker. But before Miss Thing could respond, I heard Drew's voice in the background. He said something to her about answering his phone and then the phone hung up.

"OH HELL NO!" I shouted as I redialed his number. The first time, no one picked up. I called back. This time, Drew picked up on the third ring.

"Yo'."

"Yo'? Really, Drew? You just gonna pick up all cool like a bitch didn't just answer your phone?" I screamed into the phone. This nigga had some nerve.

"Yo', chill out. That's just my home girl, Lisa. It ain't even nothing like that," he responded.

"Okay, and is this so-called home girl of yours the reason that I haven't seen or heard from you in like three days? Matter fact, who the fuck is Lisa anyway? I never met a home girl of yours named Lisa. You must think I'm stuck on stupid." I was beyond heated. Just because I was young didn't mean I was dumb.

"Look, I ain't about to argue with you tonight, V. I had a long practice today and I'm tired, so I'll holla at you tomorrow when you got your mind right." CLICK.

I looked at my phone, stunned. This nigga had the nerve to hang up on me. I didn't even bother to call back this time. I would deal with his ass tomorrow and that was a fact.

****

The next day after school, I told my mother I was tutoring, but I planned to do a pop-up visit at Drew's to confront him about last night. Today was the only day of the week he didn't have practice, so I knew he would be home, playing his stupid ass PlayStation. I made sure I was looking on point that day with Seven jeans, a crisp white baby tee, and my fresh all white Air Maxes. I pulled my hair up into a messy bun just the way Drew liked it and glossed my lips up really well. His ass was going to regret treating me the way he did the night before. When I got to Drew's, his older brother, Troy, was pulling up in his brand new Tahoe, music blasting like always.

"Wassup, Troy!" I yelled over the loud music.

"Wassup, V? What, you here looking for Drew? His ass is probably in there on that stupid ass game. Nigga needs to get him a job, straight up. But here, let me let you in," he said, hopping out of his truck and unlocking the door for me.

"Thanks," I said chuckling and walking into the tiny apartment.

I walked through the kitchen, towards the stairs that led to where Drew and Troy shared a bedroom. On the way up, I heard music playing, but I also could've sworn I heard moans. I brushed it off, thinking I had to be tripping. Without hesitation, I swung open Drew's door, ready to curse him out and then have some bomb ass makeup sex like we always did when we argued. What I saw instead instantly had my legs feeling like noodles and my vision feeling blurry.

Lisa, the cheerleading captain at Drew's school, was sitting on top of him, bouncing up and down on his dick like a pogo stick. Her back was facing me and the covers were wrapped around her waist. From the way her head was thrown back, I could tell that she was fully enjoying herself. I couldn't see Drew's face, but from the way he was gripping her waist, I could tell he was enjoying it too. *What the fuck.* I dropped my North Face backpack off my shoulder, onto the floor, with tears in my eyes. Lisa opened her eyes and looked back at me. When she saw it was me, she smirked. Her stopping caused Drew to look past her and directly at me. We made eye contact for about thirty seconds before Lisa sucked her teeth and began riding Drew's dick again like a mad woman. I expected him to push her off him or at least try to explain, but neither happened. Instead, he closed his eyes and continued enjoying another bitch riding him right in front of his so-called girlfriend.

I wanted to scream. I wanted to yell. I wanted to go crazy on both of their trifling asses. But, I just couldn't. Instead, I picked up my bag, tears rolling down my face and walked out of the room. On the way out, I brushed past Troy without even speaking. I was too embarrassed. I cried the entire number 28 bus ride home and then hours more once I got home until I had no tears left to cry.

Later on that night, Drew finally called me to break up with me officially. He hit me with the "It's not you, it's me, but hopefully we can be friends" line. I just responded, "Cool" and hung up. I was physically, mentally, and emotionally drained. I had allowed myself to be hurt again by yet another man that I thought loved me. I started to blame myself, but then I realized it wasn't me. Nah. I was a good, loyal girlfriend to Donte and to Drew. Drew was right; it was them. At that moment, I decided that niggas weren't shit and at some point, if you can't beat them, you gotta join them, right?

2005

Chapter 4

The break up with Drew turned me into a complete bitch and I had no problem admitting that. Everyone always told me how pretty I was with my chinky eyes, full lips, full natural shoulder-length hair and petite figure. And now that I was maturing, I was finally starting to get a little bit of ass and titties to go with my pretty face. With that being said, I was definitely starting to feel myself.

Dudes tried to holla at me everywhere I went on a day-to-day basis, but I paid them no mind. I shot all their approaches down just for the hell of it. I had no time for the games these niggas played and I damn sure wasn't about to get my heart broken again. My only focus was keeping my grades up while partying on the weekends with my girls. Life was good without a boyfriend. I just kept telling myself, *no nigga, no nonsense.*

This weekend in particular, I was on punishment for getting smart with my mother earlier in the week. The fighting between us seemed to be getting worse and worse. But even still, she allowed me to go over Mimi's crib for the night. And of course, Mimi let me go to a house party behind my mother's back. She was cool like that. I usually got super cute for parties, but tonight, I decided to keep it simple in fitted Baby Phat sweatpants that gripped my little booty just right, all-white mid top Forces, and a white tank top. I wrapped my hair up in my Fendi scarf so that I wouldn't sweat out my fresh press and curl, threw on my gold bamboo earrings, and glossed up my lips to finish my look.

As soon as I walked into the crowded party, I spotted Rich bending some chick over, giving her back shots on the dance floor. Rich was well known in the Bean. Although he wasn't very attractive, in my opinion, he could dress his ass off, dance better than most females and was always the life of the party. He had been checking for me ever since I was with Drew, but I had always just kept shit friendly between us.

Once he spotted me, he walked away from the girl he was dancing with and pulled me into him. I grinded my ass into his dick to the loud reggae music as he whispered in my ear, "You be playing, V, but I'ma make you my girl one day, watch. Oh, and you looking hella good in them sweatpants too, beautiful."

HA! I shook my head and chuckled. I heard that one before. "Yeah, OK, we'll see," I responded as I bent over and backed my ass up into him even harder. When the song was over, he grabbed my phone out of my hand and stored his number in it. I smirked at his persistence.

"That don't mean I'ma call you," I said playfully, rolling my eyes.

"You will," he responded, licking his lips and passing me back my vibrating phone. It was Mimi calling and texting me like crazy. I walked over to the bathroom where it was quieter to call her back.

"Wassup, Mimi?" I yelled over the music.

"BITCH, YO' MAMA IS ON HER WAY TO MY CRIB TO SEE IF YOU ARE HERE. SHE KEPT CALLING LOOKING FOR YOU AND WHEN I WOULDN'T GIVE YOU THE PHONE, SHE SAID SHE WAS ON HER WAY. YOU NEED TO LEAVE THAT PARTY NOW BEFORE SHE FUCK BOTH OF US UP. MEET ME AT THE CORNER. I'M ON MY WAY."

I sucked my teeth. My mother was such a fucking hater sometimes. "Aight, I'm coming now." I headed straight for the door. My crib wasn't far from Mimi's, so I knew we didn't have much time to get back before my mother would be there.

"Ayo, V, where you going? You just gonna leave without saying bye to me?" Rich yelled out of the third-floor window.

"My fault. I gotta go. My mother is tripping. I'ma text you, though," I said, speed walking towards the corner where I was meeting Mimi.

"Damn, that's wack. Well, at least let me walk you. It's late," he insisted.

"Nah, I'm good. My cousin is right there at the corner waiting for me." With that, I was out of sight and out of mind. Or so I thought…

****

Ten Months Later

After that night, Rich and I became inseparable. He was my best friend and he treated me like a queen. We did everything together and eventually, I started catching feelings for him. Rich bought me anything I wanted, gave me full access to all the money he made working part time after school and never told me no or made me feel like I came second to anything or anyone. Bitches hated on us and tried their hardest to break us up. Dudes couldn't understand why out of all the fly niggas in Boston that tried to holla at me, I had chosen Rich. But I did, and I was happy.

One hood rat chick named Keisha even went as far as to try and "take" Rich from me. Every time she would see him at parties, she would push up on him and every time she saw me, she would roll her eyes or whisper, talking shit about me to her girls. I didn't care, though. I was never the one to fight over a dude and I didn't plan to start now, especially when Rich made it clear to her and everyone else that all he saw was me. I didn't have any worries about her or any other females for that matter. But I guess she couldn't handle the rejection because one day, she called herself stepping to me in front of a crowd of people at the park we all chilled at during summer vacation. Keisha was twice my size and I wasn't a fighter by any means, but I damn sure wasn't about to let her disrespect me, especially in front of a crowd of people.

"Do we have a problem, V? You keep staring at me, so I'm coming over here to see if we have a problem." She was standing in front of me, trying to intimidate me, but I stood my ground.

"Last time I checked, you were the one with the problem, Keisha. I ain't never had no issue with you 'cause remember, I got what you want, not the other way around." She chuckled.

"Who, Rich? Don't nobody want his ass but you, girl." She and I both knew that was a bold face ass lie. Shit, everybody out there knew it was.

"OK, well then if that's the case, why would we have a problem?" I sarcastically asked her.

"We don't."

"OK, well good." I walked past her. I was done talking to her clown ass.

****

An hour later, my Nextel was blowing up. Everybody was chirping me, telling me how Keisha was up at the park talking crazy, saying she was going to beat my ass on sight. I was about tired of this bitch. I changed out of the jean skirt and wedges I had on and threw on some sweat shorts, a t-shirt, and my Air Forces. I wrapped my hair up in my silk scarf and took off all my jewelry. Just as I was heading for the bus stop, my mother pulled up.

"Where you going, little girl? Looking all bummy like you 'bout to go fight somebody." She was trying to be funny, but this shit was not a laughing matter as far as I was concerned.

"I am," I responded with a straight face.

"You are what?" She gave me a side-eye.

"I am about to go fight somebody. I'll be back."

"Oh, really? And who exactly are you going to fight? Keisha?" I had told her about how Keisha kept starting shit with me over Rich and she had already warned me that eventually, I was going to have to put her in her place. I guess the time had come.

"Yup."

"Where is she?"

"Up at the park."

"Who is she with?"

"I don't know."

"And who are you going with?"

"Myself." She shook her head.

"Get your ass in the car."

"Why?"

"I'm gonna bring you up there. You never go to fight somebody by yourself. Especially when you don't even know if they got back up or not. If you want to fight her, I'ma bring you. That way, if somebody tries to jump in, I can intervene. You might not have a big sister, but you do have a momma.

****

We parked around the corner from the park and walked over. I led the way and my mother followed behind me. As we were walking up, I spotted Keisha leaning against the ice cream truck, talking to her sister and her girls. She was so caught up in trying to be cute that she wasn't paying attention to her surroundings.

"Which one is her?" my mother asked.

"The one in the red," I responded, still heading in her direction.

"Oh my God, Victoria, she's huge. She is gonna kill you!" I didn't give a shit about what my mother was saying. I kept walking.

Everyone must've known what was up from the mean mug on my face because a crowd began to form behind me. As I got closer, Keisha finally spotted me coming and put a stupid little smirk on her face. That pissed me off even more. Without saying one word, I swung and punched her right in her face. She fell back, shattering the glass on the ice cream truck. I wrapped my hand around her hair, swung her down to the ground and proceeded to whoop her ass. Her sister attempted to jump in when she realized her sister wasn't getting any hits in, but my mother deaded that move quick. I whooped Keisha's ass until my mother heard the sirens coming and pulled me off her. After that, females knew that even though I was small, my bark most definitely matched my bite.

Chapter 5

Today was the day of my sweet sixteenth birthday party. My mom was throwing me a huge cookout in our backyard. I still had lots of running around to do to prepare for it, but instead of doing so, Rich and I were sitting in the ER at Boston Medical Center. I had told my mother that I was going shopping downtown so that she wouldn't be on my back about where I was at. The night before, one of Rich's homeboys had a huge house party at his crib. After a few wine coolers and a blunt or two, Rich and I ended up having unprotected sex in the bathroom, so, to cover both of our asses, I decided to go get a plan B pill just in case. I patted myself on the back for being responsible enough to take precautions this time around. There was no way I was ever getting back on another abortion table, so I knew I needed to be more careful.

Imagine my surprise when the nurse informed me that she couldn't give me the pill because I was already a few weeks pregnant. I laughed in her face, thinking that she had to be joking, but she wasn't. She was serious and I was beyond surprised and confused. But what surprised me even more was Rich's reaction when I told him.

"So, did they give it to you?" he asked as soon as I came out of the building.

"Nah," I mumbled, trying to walk past him and avoid eye contact.

"Huh? Why not?" He grabbed my arm. "V, stop. Talk to me. What happened? What did they say?" I could hear the genuine concern in his voice. I looked into Rich's eyes, fighting back tears. I already knew how this was about to play out. I had been here too many times before so I quickly prepared myself for the worse.

"They said that I'm already pregnant," I whispered, looking down at my feet. Rich smiled.

"I know," he said, letting go of my arm to walk towards the bus stop.

I stood there dumbfounded. *Did this nigga just say "I know"*, I thought to myself. When he finally looked back and realized I wasn't following behind him, he yelled, "Come on, V, you gonna be late for your party."

"Did I just hear you correctly? You said I know when I told you I was pregnant, right?" I needed to make sure I wasn't tripping because there was no way Rich could have known I was pregnant if I didn't even know.

"Yeah, you heard me right, but can we please just talk about this later? Today is your day baby and I want you to enjoy yourself. So, for now, let's just put all this behind us and go get fresh so we can stunt on everybody at your party. You know how we do!" He kissed me passionately on my lips and grabbed my hand to step onto the bus. I guess I could drop the subject, but only for today. After my party was over, I wanted to know just how Rich knew some shit about me that I didn't even know.

****

A few weeks later, my cousin was killed in a drive-by shooting. His death had my entire family stressing. I still hadn't told anyone that I was pregnant and I didn't plan to anytime soon. I was surprised that my nosey ass mother hadn't noticed yet, though. But as soon as the funeral was over and things started to calm down, the questions about my missed period and perky, swollen breasts began. I guess my answers and excuses weren't good enough because the very next day, she surprised the hell out of me and came home with a pregnancy test. I had no choice but to take it in front of her and of course, it instantly came back positive.

"Who, Victoria?" she asked, mean mugging the shit out of me.

I sucked my teeth. "Really, Ma? What you mean who?"

"Well, shit, the way yo' ass is always running the streets lately, you can't blame me for asking. So, again, who, Victoria?" She folded her arms over her chest and waited for me to answer.

"Rich, Ma, RICH!" I shouted. The nerve of her trying to act like I wouldn't know who I was pregnant by or some shit. I was faithful to Rich. He was my everything. Yeah, things had started off with him being the only one who was into us, but he grew on me and now he was all I could see in a room full of dudes.

"Hmmm, okay. And here I believed you when you told me that you and him were not sexually active. Can't get pregnant if you're not having sex, little girl. But what's done is done at this point, so you need to call Richard and tell him to bring his ass over here for dinner. We all need to have a longggg talk." She threw the pregnancy test at my chest and walked out of my room without saying another word.

****

"So...is there something you want to say to me?" My mother had me and Rich sitting on the couch like two little kids in big trouble. I had already warned Rich about what the topic of discussion was, so I hoped he had practiced his responses on the way to my house because my mother was definitely not letting this go easily.

"Umm, n-n-no, ma'am," Rich stuttered. I shook my head. I guess he hadn't practiced on his way over.

"Oh, really? According to the pregnancy test that Victoria took today, you have lots that you need to say to me. I'll wait." She sat the positive pregnancy test on the coffee table and waited for him to speak. Rich looked at me for answers. I shrugged my shoulders. I was just as lost as he was. I wanted to say something about the test being on the coffee table; it seemed very unsanitary to me, but I refrained.

"Um…I love your daughter?" My mother laughed. I shook my head again. *Really, Rich,* I thought to myself.

"Little boy, please! Y'all don't even know what love is. Can either of y'all asses even spell love? Try again!" I rolled my eyes. My mother was forcing it. She needed to just say whatever it was that she wanted to say instead of being an asshole. She was being hella dramatic and I was getting hella annoyed by it.

"Um…I'm ready to take care of my responsibilities?"

"You sure? Because that sounded more like a question than a statement." I sucked my teeth. *Are you fucking kidding me!* This shit was becoming torturous to listen to. Rich just kept digging himself deeper and deeper into my mother's hole with his lame ass responses.

"Yes, ma'am, I'm sure. I love Victoria and I'm gonna love my child by her too. I'm gonna give him or her everything that my father never gave to me and more." I smiled. *There we go, baby!* I looked up at my mother. She didn't seem impressed. She just looked from me to him and from him to me with her arms folded on her chest. We all sat there in silence for a few minutes until she finally spoke.

"Yeah, well, I guess we'll just have to see, now won't we? If y'all think y'all are ready to be parents, I'm not gonna stop y'all. But just know once y'all bring a child into this world, everything changes. It's no longer about y'all and it will be time to grow up immediately. So, if you sitting here saying that's what you want to do, Rich, I'm gonna give you a chance to prove it. And as far as you go, Victoria, you just remember what I told you that night in the hospital." I shook my head.

"Y'all can go eat now. Oh, and Victoria, after dinner, you need to call your father and tell him. I'm not the one breaking the news to him that he's gonna be a grandfather so soon." *Shit!*

****

I didn't even know why I was so nervous to tell my father I was knocked up. It wasn't like he could do or say shit. We barely had a relationship. But even still, I was struggling with this phone call. As the phone rang on the other end, I was praying like shit that he didn't answer. If my mother weren't sitting so close to me, I would lie and say it went to voicemail. Unfortunately, for me, he answered on the fourth ring.

"Hey, V, wassup? Everything aight?" I shook my head. It was a damn shame that he thought something was wrong just because I was randomly calling him. That said a lot about our relationship.

"Hey, daddy. Everything is fine. Are you busy right now?" I was stalling.

"Nah, not right now. I'm about to watch the game soon, though. Wassup?"

"Um, I have something to tell you, daddy…"

"OK… I'm listening…" I took a deep breath.

"I'm pregnant!" I closed my eyes and waited for him to respond.

Silence.

"Hello? Daddy?" I took the phone away from my ear to make sure the call hadn't disconnected.

"Yeah, I'm here."

"Oh, okay." This was beyond awkward.

Silence.

"So…how much do you need?" he finally asked.

"Huh?" I was lost.

"How much money do you need?" he asked again.

"Why would I need money?" I wasn't sure where he was going with this, but I didn't need shit from him. I was only telling him because my mother said I had to. If it were up to me, he would find out he was going to be a grandfather by word of mouth or whenever he decided to come around.

"Well, I'm assuming you telling me this 'cause you need money to get rid of it, right? You already made a stupid mistake by getting pregnant. I hope you don't plan on making a stupider mistake by going through with it." My mother shook her head next to me. My blood was boiling. The nerve of this nigga to even say some shit like that when he had barely done anything for me my entire life.

"Well, you know what they say about assuming, right? And no, I'm not calling 'cause I need your money, nor am I calling 'cause I need your well wishes or permission. I'm calling to let you know that you're gonna be a grandfather, that's it. And after what you just said to me, let's just hope that you turn out to be a better grandfather than you are a father." I hung the phone up. My mother stood up, shaking her head and walked out of the room. I looked over at Rich with tears in my eyes. He walked over and pulled me into his chest.

"We gon' be aight. Don't even trip. We don't need anybody but us."

2006

Chapter 6

"WHAA! WHAA! WHAAA!"

It had been two months since I gave birth to my baby girl, Aaliyah, and I still wasn't used to the sleepless nights that consisted of her screaming at the top of her lungs for hours at a time. I was exhausted. When I decided to go through with my pregnancy, I had no idea how hard this shit would be. Even though I was managing to make it through my junior year successfully, every day as a teenage mother was a struggle. It was 2 AM and I had been blowing up Rich's phone since midnight with no response. He hadn't been by to help with his daughter for two days. I needed a damn break!

"Yo'," he finally answered.

"Yo'? Nigga, don't answer me with no damn yo'! I know you can hear your daughter crying in the background. Where the hell have you been the past two days, Rich? You haven't even stopped by once to check on us. Wassup with you?" I needed answers.

"I've been chilling. I was gonna stop by tomorrow actually," he said nonchalantly. I sucked my teeth.

"Why can't you just come here now? I'm sleepy, Aaliyah won't stop crying, and my mom is at work until 7," I whined.

"I will see y'all tomorrow V, damn. I'm tired too," he responded with an attitude. I couldn't believe this nigga.

"Tired from what? I don't see you sitting up all night with OUR baby!" I snapped.

"Okay. But I did just leave a party where I was dancing and standing for hours, so I have the right to be tired too, don't you think?"

"No, nigga, I don't think! But what I do think is that your ass better be here first thing in the morning to help with OUR daughter so I can get some sleep. Oh, and bring some more pampers and wipes 'cause she's almost out."

Silence…

"Well, to be honest, that's not gonna work for me for two reasons. Number one, the new Jordans come out tomorrow so first thing in the morning, I'll be in line trying to grab them before they sell out. And number two, after I grab my Jordans, I'm gonna be broke until I get paid again next week. Can she wait until then or can your mom just grab the stuff and I'll pay her back?"

I took the phone away from my ear like it was a foreign object. This nigga couldn't be serious. I sat there patiently waiting for him to laugh and say just kidding.

Silence…

"So, you're tryna tell me you can't come watch your daughter in the morning so I can finally get some sleep because you'll be standing in line for some sneakers? Then, when you do finally show up to watch her, you won't have pampers or wipes because all of your money will be spent on those same sneakers? Is that correct?" I had to make sure I was hearing this shit correctly.

"I mean, yeah, basically, but—" CLICK.

I ended the call. I had heard enough. I cradled a still crying Aaliyah in my arms and rocked her until she finally drifted off to sleep. My tears gently landed on her innocent little face.

****

After that night, things with Rich and me only got worse. He spent less and less time around Aaliyah and me and more and more time running the streets with his bum ass friends. It was fair to say that we weren't even a couple at this point. Of course, I still loved him and wished things could work out, But it seemed the harder I tried, the less it worked.

It was my senior year and it was hard to focus on school because I spent most of my time worrying about Rich's every move. I knew he dealt with other girls, but he also told me every day that they meant nothing to him. As far as I was concerned, he was just fucking these hoes; he was going to get right back.

Today, I was slouched on one of the couches in study hall, stalking Rich's Instant Messenger. I knew his ass like the back of my hand so figuring out his password was easy. I watched his active conversations to see what I could find out.

RoRoSoFly: Hey boo, wat u up to?

A message came through from this square ass broad named Rochelle. I heard that Rich was dealing with her, but since she wasn't even from our city, I figured they were just rumors. But here was the proof. I wanted to respond on my end before he did, but I decided to play it cool and see where their conversation went.

Richer_Than_Youuu: Nuttin much...just got to the crib. Wassup wit u?

RoRoSoFly: In my last period class...I need to see u...

Richer_Than_Youuu: Lol ...oh yeah? Wat u miss a nigga or something? ☺

My blood boiled as I read along, but I held back on interfering with the conversation...For now!

RoRoSoFly: Lol ...of course baby...but we also need to talk...

Richer_Than_Youuu: I'm listening. Wassup?

No response. That pissed me off even more. I stared at my phone for ten minutes, waiting for a response and then finally...

Richer_Than_Youuu:???

RoRoSoFly: I'm pregnant. ☹

"I'm leaving for the day! Cover for me in last period if Ms. Wright starts asking for me, okay?" I whispered to Chrissy as I rushed to pack all my belongings into my North Face backpack.

"Ummm, where are you going Victoria? All rushing and shit. You OK?" Chrissy could always tell when something was wrong with me. She was more like my sister than my friend.

"I'm good. I just gotta go see about something. I'll call you later." With that, I was heading for the door. I could not wait to confront this lying nigga.

****

I damn near ran to Rich's crib. I managed to get there in twenty minutes flat since it wasn't too far from my school. I couldn't wait to confront his ass. How dare this nigga be selling me all these dreams about us getting back together and being a family when, in reality, he was out here getting the next bitch pregnant.

I knocked on Rich's door. "Hey, Ms. Susie, it's me, Victoria. Did Richard make it home from school yet?" I said sweetly to Rich's great aunt when she opened the door.

"Yes, honey, but I think he just ran out to the corner store. You can go on upstairs and wait for him if you want with yo' pretty self. I'm just in here watching my soaps. Where's that fat lil baby of yours at?" I chuckled. Ms. Susie loved her some Aaliyah.

"She's with my mom. I'll bring her by to see you this weekend," I said as I headed upstairs to Rich's bedroom. Rich was a neat freak, so I wasn't surprised to see his room clean as a whistle when I walked in. I thought about trashing his room but quickly changed my mind, knowing damn well Ms. Susie would kick my ass. She was a nice old lady, but she was crazy as hell. Then I thought about cutting up all his clothes, but I knew I didn't have time for all of that. Rich would be back from the corner store in no time. I plopped down on his bed and brainstormed all the ways I could hurt him so he could feel how I was feeling right at this moment. I took my Polo baseball cap off so my hair could breathe. DING! His hats!

Rich loved his hats and sneakers more than anything in the damn world. I opened the window in his room that faced the street and began throwing his fitted caps out one by one into the dirty street. I had already thrown out three when I peeped Rich walking up his street, talking on his cell. *He's probably on the phone with that bitch,* I thought as I continued throwing hats out the window. I figured he would've noticed what I was doing by now, but luckily for me; he was too caught up in his conversation. He headed towards the back of the house to come through the backdoor instead of the front where his window was. A minute later, I heard him walk into the apartment.

"Hey, Ma, I got you some ice cream from the store," he said to Ms. Susie. She was the only mother he had ever known.

"Oh, thank you, baby! You know grape nut is my favorite. Victoria's upstairs waiting for you. She said she's gonna bring that sweet lil baby by to see me this weekend since you never do," she said, rolling her eyes. Rich walked into his room and found me sitting on his bed, arms crossed, smirking like a little kid hiding a secret.

"Wassup, V? What you doing here so early? Shouldn't you still be in school?" he asked with a confused look.

"Don't ask wassup, Rich. Try asking what's down," I chuckled.

"Yo', what the fuck are you talking about, girl? I'm not in the mood for no riddles today, so whatever you tryna say, just say the shit, please. I need to do my homework and lay down so I can get my mind right."

"Oh, trust me, neither am I. I'm in no mood at all. But I do suggest that you go over to your window and look down. Oh, and hats off to your new pregnancy," I threw in as I got up to leave.

I knew once he saw his hats scattered all over the street being run over by cars it was going to be war. I got halfway down his street before I looked back to see him charging up the street, screaming my name.

"BITCH, ARE YOU FUCKING CRAZY?! WHAT THE FUCK IS WRONG WITH YOU?!" he yelled, enraged.

"Yeah, actually, I am crazy! And you clearly are too, nigga! Our daughter is six months old and you already got the next bitch pregnant! You fucking right that shit got me feeling crazy!" I screamed back in his face.

"So what! We are NOT together! I do what the fuck I want!" I could tell I had proven my point and pissed him off to the extreme. I was satisfied with that for now, so I turned to walk away before shit could get any worse. He wasn't done, though.

"You ain't shit but a whole bunch of drama! I swear I regret ever getting yo' ass pregnant. Real shit. I wish your ass were dead."

Without even thinking, I instantly turned around and punched him in his mouth and then I just stood there, ready for whatever came next. I watched as blood slowly began to trickle down his lip. He wiped it with the back of his hand, never taking his eyes off me. His eyes were filled with so much hate that I started getting nervous and decided I better leave now before he reacted to what I had just done. But before I could move, he was charging at me, placing his hand around my throat. Luckily, one of his homeboys peeped the whole scene and was already on his way across the street to separate us. One of his other homeboys followed his lead by coming over and grabbing me by the arm and dragging me to the bus stop to leave. He knew I was in fight mode so he wouldn't leave until I boarded the bus. As soon as the bus pulled off, I heard sirens in the area. I knew Rich's aunt had called the cops on us and I was sure she had called my mother by now as well. I sat back in my seat and mentally prepared myself for round two when I got home.

Chapter 7

As soon as I walked into my house, the look on my mother's face told me that she had already spoken to Rich's aunt. She was sitting on the couch, arms crossed, waiting for my arrival. I wanted to turn around and walk right back out the door, but I knew that wasn't an option. I would have to face her eventually unless I planned on moving out and leaving all my shit there. And even then, she would still probably make it her business to confront me wherever I was.

"Hey, Ma!" I tried to avoid eye contact and keep walking towards my room, but she wasn't having it.

"Hey, ma, my ass! You already know why I'm sitting here like this so don't even try it, Victoria. What the hell is wrong with you going to people's house acting a damn fool! I know I raised you better than that!" I rolled my eyes.

"I don't know what you talking about." I had already decided on my bus ride home that I was going to deny ever being there. That was my story and I planned to stick to it. As far as I was concerned, she wasn't there, which meant that she couldn't prove that I was.

"Oh OK, so you just gonna lie right in my face now? That's how we're doing it now?" At this point, she was now standing and we were toe to toe. She was so close to my face that I could feel her breath as she spoke. I knew I needed to back down before shit got ugly, but I was still pissed about the way things had just gone down with Rich. I was in no mood for my mother's bullshit.

"Well, if you want to get technical, I'm not doing anything, you are, and I'm not in yo' face, you in mine, and I really wish you weren't right now."

WHAP!

My mother slapped me across my face before I could even finish my sentence. I stood there holding my cheek, stunned. As many times as she had threatened to, she had never actually slapped me before. I was boiling on the inside as I thought about charging at her ass, but the look in her eyes told me I would regret that move; so I stood there, mean mugging her instead.

"I wish you would," she said through gritted teeth. She must've read my mind. I shook my head and attempted to turn and walk away. She grabbed my backpack before I could.

"I'm not done with you, little girl. Matter fact, sit yo' grown ass over there on the couch." I plopped down on the couch, rolling my eyes. I wish she would just yell at me and get it over with. There was no need for a long drawn out conversation or lecture. Whatever my punishment was, I accepted it with open arms. I honestly just wanted to be left alone.

"Rich's aunt called me and told me what happened today. She didn't know the details of what happened exactly, but what she did describe to me was enough for me to know that you must have lost yo' mind. What the hell would make you think that it was okay to show up to that woman's house and act crazy like yo' momma didn't teach you any home training? I know you and Rich have been on and off since Aaliyah got here, but that gives you no right to just show up at his house, toss his belongings into the streets and then put yo' damn hands on him. You just told me the other day that you wanted to work things out with him. This is not working things out, Victoria."

"Fuck him! I ain't working shit out with his bitch ass!" I shouted at the top of my lungs. Just hearing his name had me heated and ready to fight again.

"Oh, you must want to get slapped again, huh? You better watch yo' damn mouth! You are not grown!" For a minute, I had forgotten who I was talking to. I quickly calmed myself down.

"My bad."

"Yeah, I know it is your bad. Now what the hell could that boy have done that was that bad that you doing all this extra stuff that you did today? Especially when your ass was still supposed to be in school."

"Why don't you ask him?" I rolled my eyes.

"I'm asking you. He's not my child, you are. And if you roll yo' eyes at me or get smart one more damn time, I'ma knock them shits in the back of your head and then punch you in yo' flip ass mouth." I could still feel the sting on my cheek from where she slapped me. I didn't want any problems, so I apologized.

"Sorry. I just honestly don't feel like talking about any of this right now, please. I just want to do my homework and go to bed." What I really planned to do was snoop some more on Rich's accounts to see what was up with him and Rochelle.

"OK, fine, but we will be talking about this tomorrow and you will be calling Rich's aunt to apologize for yo' behavior. But let me just say this to you; ain't a man in this world worth your pride and dignity, you hear me? Don't you ever lower yourself to some ghetto, drama-filled hood rat in the street for ANY man. You're better than that. If Rich doesn't wanna do the right thing, let his ass go. It'll be his loss. Now, go wake up Aaliyah from her nap before you start yo' homework, or she's gonna have you up all night."

Once I finished all my homework and got Aaliyah settled for bed, I flipped open my pink sidekick phone. I was hoping to see a missed call or text from Rich, but there was nothing but a text from Chrissy, asking if I was okay. I texted her back saying I was okay and proceeded to sign into Rich's instant messenger account. The little green dot next to his screen name let me know that he was active, which meant he was probably having a conversation with someone on his end. Before I could finish my thought, my phone vibrated, letting me know that I had a message. I opened my notifications and saw that it was a response to Rich's screen name from the screen name *YaYa_PrettyGurl*. *Bingo!* I opened the conversation and read.

YaYa_PrettyGurl: Okay, but why would she even show up acting like that if y'all ain't fucking with each other no more? Why are people telling me it had something to do with another chick, Rich? I'm not stupid, so you need to just tell me the truth.

I shook my head. This nigga Rich was the definition of an ain't shit nigga. Not only did he have some bitch pregnant, he had another bitch thinking she was his number one too. Less than a minute later, Rich responded.

Richer_Than_Youuu: Idk why her ass showed up. I keep telling you she's crazy. She wants me back but I ain't even fucking with her like that. I just take care of my seed. You my only girl. You know that.

I had to laugh out loud at that shit. Rich had literally fucked me less than a week ago, yet here he was saying he wasn't "fucking with me like that." Then he had the nerve to say all he did was take care of his seed, yet he hadn't done shit for Aaliyah in over a month. *This nigga is a fucking joke,* I thought to myself.

YaYa_PrettyGurl: Okay, so if I'm yo' only girl, why am I hearing that you been messing with some chick named Rochelle?

Richer_Than_Youuu: I don't know no Rochelle...you know people be lying. Trying to come between what we got.

I signed off Rich's screen name and back on to my own. I had seen enough. This nigga was playing all types of games with me, Rochelle, and whoever the hell this other chick was. I wasn't even mad anymore. I was just glad that I finally saw things for what they were. Rich could do him and I damn sure was going to do me from this point on. Just to be an asshole, I put up an away message directed towards him, knowing he'd see it since he was signed on.

FUCK niggas. Get MONEY...Especially UGLY niggas...Fuck them twice! Single and Loving it!

Twenty minutes later, who was calling me, all in their feelings? Rich, of course. I almost didn't answer, but I wanted to see what this clown I had to say for himself.

"Yeah, who's this?" I answered, acting like I didn't know who it was.

"Victoria, please girl. You know exactly who it is. Even if you erased my number, you still know my shit by heart and that's a fact, so save the act." His matter of fact attitude was pissing me off.

"Look, what the fuck do you want, Richard? I'm busy and ain't got time to talk to unimportant people." I wasn't doing shit but lying in my bed, watching TV, but he didn't need to know that.

"You ain't doing shit, but OK. I just called to say that shit you did today was mad corny and childish. I can't deal with nobody who acts like that over nothing. You cut, yo'." I burst out laughing. Was this nigga serious?

"I'm cut?" I said through laughter.

"Yeah, you're cut. I'm all set on you yo" He was serious. That made me laugh even more.

"OK, Rich. Is that all?" I was done entertaining this fool for the night. He must've felt some kind of way about me laughing because before I could say anything else, he hung up. Still laughing, I switched my lamp and TV off and turned over to go to bed for school in the morning. I was going to sleep well knowing that I got the last laugh.

Chapter 8

The situation with Rochelle and the other chick sealed the deal between me and Rich. But even still, there was no way I was going to allow him to have another baby so soon and have me looking stupid. After I threatened Rochelle about how miserable I would make her and Rich's life if she even considered keeping his baby, she eventually made the decision to get rid of it. One day, I even told her, "If you don't go get rid of it, I'll get rid of it for you." I know that's fucked up, but hey, I needed her to know that I wasn't playing any games. The way I saw it, I was doing her and Rich a favor. Rich barely took care of Aaliyah, so what the fuck was he going to do with another baby other than abandon that one too? The real icing on the cake was when I gave Rochelle a shoulder to cry on after she had her abortion. Of course, I only did this to spite Rich. And of course, Rochelle's dumb ass fell for it; she'd much rather have me as a "friend" than an enemy.

"Why are you chilling with that girl, Victoria? You know damn well you don't like her," my mother asked me one night at the dinner table.

"It's simple. If I can't have Rich, neither can she. Plus, she likes to party, so she's cool with me for now," I responded, shrugging my shoulders.

"Yeah, well, she also doesn't have a baby to take care of, which gives her every right to party uninterrupted. But you, on the other hand, do, which is why you need to slow yo' little hot ass down." I rolled my eyes. This was a constant argument between us nowadays. I don't know why she even cared, considering the fact her ass never babysat Aaliyah when I did go out. But, to avoid the drama, I didn't even bother to respond.

"And quite frankly, why do you even give a damn about what Rich is doing? As far as I'm concerned, a nigga that goes out and gets the next girl pregnant, but ain't even taking care of his first one, deserves no time or attention from you. You're better than that, Victoria. When are you gonna learn to just worry about you and yo' daughter, little girl?" I hated when she called me that shit and she knew it. I wanted to tell her I'd learn as soon as she learned to mind her damn business and call me by my name and not little girl, but after our last argument, I knew better.

I sat there in silence, picking at my food.

"I guess that means never, huh?" She shook her head.

"I'm not really hungry, can I please be excused? I need to study for my exam tomorrow." I tried to sound as polite as possible. She looked at me and shook her head again.

"Go right ahead, Victoria."

****

It was New Year's Eve and Rochelle and I were about to hit the streets of Boston and act up. My older cousin, Tanya, had agreed to babysit Aaliyah, so her house was our first stop for the night. As soon as we pulled up on her street in Rochelle's Nissan Altima, I spotted Rich outside with his homeboys, drinking and smoking. They were being so loud and rowdy that they didn't even notice us when we pulled up and parked.

Rochelle stepped out first. I had to keep it real; she wasn't an ugly girl at all. She was about the same size as me in build, except I had a little more booty. She was a dark caramel complexion with hair that was all hers and hung past her shoulders, and she had chinky eyes just like me. Tonight, she had on cut-off Levi jean shorts, a black tank top with a black Guess blazer and matching black Guess leather pumps. She had pulled her hair up in a cute messy bun with bangs.

"Damn, wassup, Rochelle?" Rich said, licking his lips. She blushed. She couldn't even hide her excitement from him noticing her, but before she could respond, I slowly opened the passenger side door and stepped out. Rich's mouth instantly dropped to the floor. I had on a tight fitting mini BCBG tank dress with a fitted black leather jacket and red, strappy BCBG six-inch stilettos. I never wore much makeup since I was naturally pretty, but tonight, I finished my look off with a red lip and some mascara to enhance my already full lashes. My eighteen-inch weave hung down my back in loose curls. I knew I was the shit and at that moment, Rochelle, Rich, and all his boys knew I was the shit too.

"Hey, y'all." I waved as I strutted by with Aaliyah on my hip.

"Really, V?" Rich said in an annoyed tone.

"Really, what?" I acted dumbfounded. If he wanted to play games, I could play them too.

"Number one, where is the rest of yo' dress at? Number two, I know you see me standing here, so next time, speak, and number three, where the hell do you think you are going with her?" He pointed at Rochelle, who was standing in one place, looking nervous as hell. I chuckled.

"Hmmm, lemme see. At the store, didn't even notice you, and minding our business." I winked at him and motioned for Rochelle to follow me to my cousin's door. Rich grabbed my arm.

"Victoria, don't fucking play with me, yo'. Where are you going in this little ass dress?" I snatched away.

"Um, the last time I checked, I was very much single. Don't you gotta bitch or something like that?" No answer.

"Exactly! So worry about her and please remove your hands off what no longer belongs to you. This right here is for REAL niggas only, lame! THANKS!" And with that, I walked away. I could hear his boys laughing and clowning him behind me. Talk about a checkmate! Here he was sweating me, yet he never even bothered to acknowledge his own damn daughter. Pathetic!

****

Later on that night, Rich ended up at the same after party as us. He was pissy drunk and all over me as soon as he spotted me. I looked over and peeped Rochelle in the corner fake smiling at us, but I was no dummy. I knew she secretly wished that she were me at that moment. She still liked Rich and if she could, she would be with him. But I wasn't having it, which was why I kept her right under my wing where I could monitor her. I decided to take Rich outside to try to sober him up a little with some fresh air.

"V, I got something to tell you, yo'," he slurred.

"Rich, you're mad drunk. You don't have anything to tell me that you're actually gonna remember saying tomorrow, so save it, please," I responded, rolling my eyes.

"Nah, for real. This is real talk. I still love you, yo'. I want us to try and make it work for Aaliyah." He damn near fell trying to pull me in closer to him. I pushed him away. This nigga had me fucked up. Today was the first day of a new year. My daughter was a few months short of being one year old and I was finally starting to get used to the thought of us not being together. Even if I was blocking Rochelle from being with him, there was still no way I was letting him pull me back onto his emotional rollercoaster. Not this time.

"Like I said, you're drunk, Rich. You don't even know what you saying. You ain't been thinking about me, so don't let the

Henny make you start now." That's what my mouth said, but deep down in my heart, I was wishing all that he was saying was what he really felt. But, I knew that it wasn't, so I stood firm in my decision.

"Yo', you gotta believe me. I love you, yo'." He leaned in to kiss me and before I could move away, he vomited all down the front of my dress and on my red suede stilettos.

"URGGHHHH! What the fuck, Rich! Damn man!" I screamed. One of his boys heard the commotion and came running outside to see what was up.

"Get yo' fucking boy, yo', 'cause I'm all the way done with his ass!" I yelled, pushing Rich to the ground in his own vomit. I walked away, back into the house to find Rochelle. She was all up in some nigga's face that I'm sure she barely knew. I snatched her by the arm and told her it was time to go.

"But we just got here," she whined.

"Yeah, and now we're leaving!" I shouted over the loud music.

I could tell she was disappointed, but she wouldn't dare challenge me. And if she did, she would look up and be there all by herself because I was leaving with or without her at this point. And I wasn't waiting either. She said her goodbyes to whomever the dude was she was talking to and we headed for the door. On the way out, I looked over to the side of the house where Rich's boys were trying to get his drunk ass off the ground. I shook my head, promising myself that I would never ever look back that way.

Chapter 9

And I didn't. Instead, I tried my hardest to put all my focus into school and Aaliyah. For a while, it worked. My life basically consisted of going to school and then going to work and then going home to be a mom. But even still, it seemed as though somehow, someway, every ain't shit dude in Boston managed to fall right into my lap, literally. I wasn't looking for companionship at this point, but I must've had the words "play me" written in big bold letters on my forehead.

First, there was Louis, who I met while working part-time as a peer leader at my local community center. He worked there too and always flirted with me every chance he got. Louis was half-Spanish–half-Black, with a sexy caramel complexion, perfect white teeth and waves that could make any female seasick. He was also a comedian, so he kept us laughing all day at work. When I finally did decide to give him a chance, I soon found out that he was freakier than he was funny. Just the way I liked it.

Louis brought out my adventurous side when it came to sex. He was down to do it anywhere. Parks, stores, subway stations on the late night. You name it, he was down for it and I was more than willing to follow his lead. He even had me sneaking in his basement one day while his dad was right upstairs with his friends, having beers. The excitement of trying to stay quiet while he banged my back out with no mercy had me dripping wet.

"Arch that back and stop playing, girl!" he whispered, thrusting himself in and out of me as I held on to his father's pool table for dear life. It was taking everything in me not to scream out in ecstasy.

"Urgghhh. I can't, baby. It feels tooo gooodd. What are you doing to me?" I could feel myself about to explode as my legs started getting weaker with each thrust. He chuckled.

"Can't ain't in a real woman's vocabulary. Now take this dick!" He started thrusting even faster and harder as my legs began to shake. Just as I was about to reach my peak, he pulled out, picked me up, sat my bare, wet ass on the edge of the pool table and started eating it. Two seconds later, my eyes were rolling in the back of my head as my body convulsed and my juices flowed all over his face.

That was the kind of shit that happened daily. There was never a dull moment with Louis and I loved that about him. Unlike my previous relationships, Louis and I were taking things one day at a time and having fun while doing it. I genuinely enjoyed my time with him and looked forward to our future together. But, of course, everything that glitters ain't gold and every nigga that seems perfect ain't real.

One day, Aaliyah and I went to meet Louis and his two-year-old son, Anthony, for ice cream. We often had play dates with our kids and that was another thing that I was feeling about Louis. Well, to both of our surprise, Louis' dad, who I had only met twice since we'd been dating, happened to be at the same ice cream shop buying an iced coffee before work. Anthony spotted him first and instantly starting screaming, "Papi! Papi!" while running over to where he was. I was lost.

"Um, why is YOUR son calling YOUR dad, daddy? Isn't that a little weird?" I asked, completely confused by what I just witnessed, but not wanting to judge or assume.

"Ummm. Nah, it's not weird at all. He's just a kid. He calls him what he hears me call him, that's all. Plus, in our culture, papi can be dad or granddad." What he was saying made sense, but I could tell he was getting nervous as his father headed to our table with Anthony on his hip. He greeted me with a fake smile. I knew his father didn't like me much from the first time I met him. Probably because I was a little Black ghetto girl from the hood and not Spanish like him. That was his problem, though. I was still going to fuck his son when I wanted to.

"Hey, son, you didn't tell me you were taking your brother out for ice cream today. What time did you guys leave the house?" he said to Louis, who now had his head down.

"Brother?" I mumbled under my breath. I looked over at Louis, waiting for him to correct his father. He never even looked up; instead, he kept his head down while answering his dad's question. That was all I needed to see to know that what his dad had just said was the truth. I excused myself from the table, grabbed Aaliyah and her diaper bag and headed straight for the door. I was all set. What kind of person pretends that their sibling is their child just to impress a female that has a child of her own? He even went as far as to have the little boy call him daddy when I was around. Where they do that at?

Weeks later, after I finally got Louis to stop blowing up my phone, trying to explain himself and get me back, I met Kareem through some mutual friends. I fucked him on the very first night that we chilled and I should've known from that alone that our "relationship" would be short-lived. We fucked any and everywhere damn near every day for about a month or so. I met his mother once, but he never even made it far enough to meet mine or even Aaliyah, for that matter. As soon as I mentioned wanting more than just sex with him, what we had was over before it even began. It didn't matter to me, though. All I would miss about Kareem was his big ole hook-shaped dick and all the great sex we had; nothing more, nothing less. I just told myself that it was fun while it lasted.

Last but not least, there was Chris, who was a family friend that turned into more out of nowhere. I really, really liked Chris and could actually see myself having a future with him. He adored Aaliyah and me and would do anything I asked of him, except commit to an actual relationship. I mean, it's kind of hard to commit to one female when you're secretly juggling three, right? This nigga had females prank calling my phones and some more shit. I had no time to be fighting over a nigga that wasn't even officially mine, so I had to fall back from that situation quickly. I was not trying to catch a case for fucking up a bitch. It wouldn't look good on my college applications.

Eventually, I just had to say fuck all these niggas and go back to being that good girl that everyone around me thought I was anyway. Of course, I still thought about Rich every single day, even though I had clearly moved on. I thought about what we could've been and how us not being together would affect Aaliyah in the long run. But at seventeen, I had already had my heart broken enough times. My heart had become cold and my pussy had become loose.

It wasn't until Rich called me one day talking shit that I realized that it was time to reel myself in for the sake of my daughter because soon, she would be watching and hearing everything.

"What do you want, Rich? Ain't you supposed to be on yo' way here to pick Aaliyah up? Don't sound like you are."

"Nah. I'm not."

"Oh? And why aren't you? You know I'm supposed to be working tomorrow morning." It was always some bullshit when it came to Rich taking care of his daughter.

"Yeah, I know, but I'll come get her in the morning. I need to clear my head tonight. I had a rough ass day today." I laughed.

"Rough ass day? Nigga, you don't even work anymore. All your ass did was go to school, if you even did that!" Rich killed me with his dramatics.

"Yeah, I did go to school and while I was there, I had to sit back and hear about how I got a hoe for a baby momma."

"Excuse me?" Oh yeah, this nigga was tripping.

"Yeah, you heard me. I had to sit back and listen while yo' boys, Donte and Drew, clowned each other back and forth at lunch about who had you first. And when I tried to defend you, niggas started going in on me about how I was stupid enough to actually have a baby with you." I had heard enough. All of what he was saying sounded like some real little kid shit.

"Look, don't ever feel like you need to defend me 'cause trust and believe, I'm good. I don't give a fuck about what bitch ass Donte or Drew has to say about me. Them niggas don't pay my bills, take care of my daughter, or pass my tests for me in school. And to be honest, if I wanted them back, I could have them, just like I could have you. So, if you wanna get caught up in the dumb shit and feel some kinda way, that's fine, but that does not mean you don't get to be a father. So, get yo' ass over here and get yo' daughter so I can work tomorrow to provide for her since you can't!" I slammed the phone down.

I couldn't even act like all that Rich had just told me surprised me. Especially since Donte and Drew had both tried on numerous occasions to see if they could have another chance with me. I turned them both down every time so the bitterness was expected. It was a known fact that people always hate when they can't have what they want. Rich should've known that. Even so, it was still definitely time to slow my ass down.

Chapter 10

I had just got off the number 16 bus at Forest Hills Station when my stomach started to rumble. I wasn't too surprised, considering the fact that I had skipped lunch at school and only ate a Pop-Tart out of the vending machine at work. It was now 6 PM and I was starving. I decided to walk over to the pizza shop since my next bus home wasn't coming for another twenty minutes. I stood at the crosswalk, waiting for someone to let me cross when I heard someone call my name. I turned and looked; it was my best friend, Toya. She was getting out of a car. *That car looks familiar as shit,* I thought to myself. I stopped in my tracks and waited for her to get to where I was.

"Hey, bitch, you look cute or whatever. Where you coming from?" We embraced each other, but my eyes were still glued to the car pulling off and making a U-turn in the middle of the street. I would've been able to see who was driving, but the tints in the window prevented that.

"Um, helloooo. I asked you a question."

"Oh, um, my bad. I'm coming from work. I was about to go get a slice from the pizza shop. I'm fucking starving. Where you coming from?"

"Oh okay. I'll walk with you. I'm starving too."

"Where you coming from?" I asked again as we proceeded with crossing the street.

"Oh, nowhere important. Just a friend's house." Her answer seemed a little vague, so I pried.

"Oh okay. Who was that that dropped you off? For some reason, that car looked mad familiar." She looked away.

"Oh, that was just Kareem." She was damn near whispering, so I figured I had heard her wrong.

"Who?"

"Kareem."

"Kareem, who?"

I already knew what Kareem she was talking about, but I needed to be sure.

"Kareem, Kareem."

"Kareem, my Kareem?" I asked, giving her the side-eye. She rolled her eyes.

"Well, he's not really *your* Kareem, but yeah, that Kareem."

"Um, yes, he is my Kareem. I was the one fucking him, remember?" Now I was getting pissed off.

"Yeah, I remember," she said nonchalantly.

"Okay, so what were you doing in his car then if you remember?" I guess now I knew why the car looked so familiar. I had fucked Kareem in that car on numerous occasions and Toya, of all people, knew this.

"Damn bitch, I already told you. He was giving me a ride from my friend's house. Why you asking all these damn questions? Interrogating me and shit." She was getting defensive. That told me she was hiding something.

"Okay, but I don't understand how that would even happen. Y'all don't even know each other outside of me and I haven't fucked with him in months, so how are y'all even in contact?" This shit was not adding up to me whatsoever.

"We ain't in contact, if you must know. I was standing at the bus stop and he happened to drive by. He saw me, so he stopped and offered me a ride. I don't even know why you're forcing it right now, to be honest. It's not like he was ever even your man like that or anything." I looked at her like she had lost her damn mind.

"No, he was never my man, but I was fucking him on a regular basis, so it's the fucking principle, Toya." I was yelling now and everyone in the pizza shop was looking at me like I was crazy. I lowered my voice.

"Are you fucking with him?" I looked her in her eyes to see if she was lying when she responded.

"No, bitch! I don't want yo' recycled dick! For the last damn time, he only gave me a ride here and it only happened by chance. It wasn't planned. Now get off my back, damn!" I stared at her hard. She looked like she was telling the truth, but something in my gut told me she wasn't being completely honest. Either way, she kind of had a point about him never being my man, so I decided to let it go. If she did in fact sleep with him, I would find out eventually. Boston was too small for me not to. That was a proven fact.

✱✱

That weekend, Toya and I continued with our regularly scheduled program as if the little falling out about Kareem had never even happened. That's why she was my bestie. It was never any love lost with us. It was a nice day out, so we decided to put Aaliyah in the stroller and head to the Galleria mall to grab the new Jordans that came out that morning. We walked into

Footlocker, laughing and joking about some ugly boy on the trolley that had tried to touch Toya's big ole booty on the low, when I noticed some girl over on the other side of the store, grilling me. I didn't recognize her, so I brushed it off, thinking maybe she was looking past me and not at me.

We were waiting for the sales associate to bring out our sizes so we could try them on when Toya tapped me on the shoulder and nodded in the girl's direction that I had noticed before.

"You know her?"

"Nah. You?"

"Nope, but what I do know is that she done had an eye problem since we walked into this store. And if she doesn't fix it soon, I'm gonna fix that shit for her." Toya was always ready to lay a bitch out. We were total opposites in that sense. I preferred to keep it cool until somebody pushed me to do otherwise.

"Yeah, I noticed too, but I thought maybe I was tripping." I looked over at the girl again and she was still mean mugging. Toya stood up.

"I'm 'bout to go say something." I pulled her back down onto the bench.

"Nah chill, we got Aaliyah with us. We can't be in this mall fighting and shit. That bitch can stare all she wants; long as that's all she does, she's good."

Toya sucked her teeth, rolled her eyes, and tried on her sneakers. After we both had made sure we had the correct sizes, we headed to the front of the store. As we were walking towards the register, the mystery girl was walking away, bag in hand. As she walked past me, she purposely let her sneaker bag hit me in my leg. I stopped in my steps and looked back.

"Excuse you," I said with much attitude.

"No, bitch, excuse yo' wack ass." Okay, so this bitch did want problems. Toya jumped in her face before I could even respond.

"What the fuck you say to my best friend, bitch? Ya bum ass better keep it pushing before you get fucked up in this store." To my surprise, the mystery girl didn't back down. Instead, she chuckled in Toya's face. I could tell by her appearance alone that she was a roughneck type chick. She looked like she had been fighting all her life, but it was whatever. If she wanted to take it there, we could.

"I don't even know who the fuck you are, or what yo' issue with me is, but if you ever get in my space again, I will fuck you up, bitch. So, speak on the problem or keep it moving." I had to let her know that this shit was not a game, so I started removing my earrings before she could even respond. *Thank God, I wore sneakers today*. She stood there, shaking her head at me.

"Look at you taking your earrings out, ready to fight, just like the hood rat Rich said you were. You don't even care that you got yo' daughter with you. Ha! No wonder he doesn't wanna be with your ass." I died laughing.

"So, that's with this is about? Rich? Girl, ain't nobody thinking about his ass. I've been done with him. But, for the record, I'm far from a hood rat, boo. If you wanna get technical, I'm just protecting my child and you the hood rat for even tryna pop off while I have my child with me. But because I now know that this is over Rich, me and my girl right here are gonna give you a pass. But if you ever step to me again, I promise you you're gonna regret it." We stood there toe to toe, staring each other down until she finally spoke.

"Yeah, okay. We'll see about that."

"Yeah, I'm sure we will. What's yo' name anyway? I mean, you clearly know who I am, but I didn't even know you existed. Especially since Rich is still sniffing up my ass." Me and Toya gave each other a high five and started laughing.

"My name is Ayanna. Remember it, bitch, 'cause this won't be the last of me you'll see." She turned and walked away. I wasn't sure what that last comment meant, but I wasn't tripping. All I could do was thank God that I had left Rich alone when I did because if he was bringing me this kind of drama while we were apart, I could only imagine the drama I'd be in if we were still together.

2007

Chapter 11

I breezed through the remainder of my senior year with no more boyfriends, hardly any sex, but lots of partying. I managed to graduate and score a full scholarship to any state school based on how good I did on my MCAS exams. I also got into a few other colleges, but because I had Aaliyah, I took advantage of the free money and decided that staying home for school was what was best for now.

It was the summer before my freshman year in college. I was finally turning eighteen in a few days and I was most definitely feeling myself more than usual. I decided to take a quick trip to Atlanta for my birthday weekend with Toya. Partying in Boston had gotten completely played out at this point. It was always the same people at every party. I wanted to meet new people and experience life outside of Boston. I was surprised that my mother agreed to let me go, but when she said yes, I knew that it was best that I didn't ask any questions.

"Girl, who's picking us up again? Your cousin, right?" I asked in an annoyed tone. Waiting on people was one of my biggest pet peeves. Patience was something I just didn't have and if I knew the address of where I was going, I would have been flagged a taxi to take me to my destination.

"Yes, V, for the last damn time, girl. My cousin Q is picking us up and we're staying at his crib for the weekend," Toya responded just as annoyed.

"Q and V. That sounds good together, don't it? I hope his ass is as cute as you claim he is. I haven't had no dick in forever and at least if I give him some, I don't gotta deal with him once we leave. Real life hit it and quit it!" I laughed at my own joke.

"You're a fucking mess, I swear! But yes, girl, my cousin is most definitely a cutie. Shit, if he wasn't blood, I would probably… Oh wait, there he go right there! Q!" She waved her hand in the air to get his attention. I glanced in the direction that she was waving in and had to rub my eyes to make sure I was seeing correctly. Q was not a cutie, that nigga was FINE! He was about six feet tall, light skin, with a slender build and a low fade. He had deep dimples on both sides of his well-groomed face when he smiled. He kind of reminded me of the rapper T.I. at first sight. Even in his simple grey Nike sweat suit and fresh white Air Force Ones, he looked sexy as shit. I wanted him instantly.

"Hey, Toya! Sorry I'm late, shawty. This Atlanta traffic crazy this time of day." He was talking to her, but staring at me. His slight southern accent had my kitty cat dripping wet. I didn't even realize how hard I was staring back until he finally broke our gaze by speaking directly to me.

"Hey, lil mama, nice to finally meet you. I'm Quincy. What yo' name is?" he asked, licking his lips and smiling. I swear I came on myself at that exact moment.

"Hiiiii," was all I could muster up to say back, cheesing like a complete idiot. Toya rolled her eyes and nudged me in my arm.

"Damn girl! Close yo' mouth and stop drooling already! Q, this is V. V, this is Q. Now, can you grab our bags so we can get up outta this airport? I'm starving."

I stayed quiet during the whole ride to Q's apartment complex. He lived in one of the more urban parts of Atlanta and as soon as we walked into his actual apartment, I knew it was a trap house. For some strange reason, that made me want him even more. I loved a nigga that was about his paper; however he got it was his business. Toya and I both showered and changed out of our comfortable traveling clothes into outfits that were more appropriate for the day's activities. Q told us he would be taking us to the Stonecrest Mall to shop first and then to Gladys Knight's Chicken and Waffle to eat afterward. The whole time we were out and about, Q and I flirted with each other nonstop.

"Aye, V, yo' fries over there looking good as shit. Let me get one." I wanted to tell him his fine ass could have more than my fries, but I played it cool.

"Help yourself. I ain't gonna eat all of this food anyway." I pushed my plate towards him, across the table.

"Nah, I want you to feed it to me," he said with a sly grin. If these were the kind of games he wanted to play, he most definitely had the right one. I grabbed the longest fry I could find, leaned across the table and headed towards his mouth with it. Just as it touched the tip of his lips, I stopped and stuck the entire fry into my mouth, along with my finger that I then sucked clean, never taking my eyes off him. He bit down on his bottom lip; I knew what that meant. I decided right at that moment that I was definitely fucking him before I left Atlanta. No questions asked.

The second night we were there, we stayed in at Q's crib and had our own little party instead of going to the club. Q invited over a few of his homeboys and everyone drank and smoked and had a good time.

"Damn Toya, where's the rest of yo' shorts at?" I asked, rolling my eyes. Her ass was beginning to work my last nerve. If I didn't know any better, I would say we were in competition for her cousin's attention. Of course, I was winning, but that was besides the fact. I hated females who constantly felt like they had to be the center of attention, especially during MY birthday weekend.

"These are the only pajama shorts I packed. Don't be mad you ain't got all this ass, boo!" She twerked her fat ass in a circle, damn near bouncing it on her cousin's shoulder as she walked past the couch he was sitting on. I shook my head. Toya never had a chill button and neither did her pussy, so I couldn't even act like I was too surprised by the way she was acting. Instead, I just brushed it off and continued plotting on how I was going to get Q's fine ass alone before we left in two days.

I looked over at the expression on his face and was sure that I wasn't the only one who noticed Toya's unnecessary extraness. Q was making a face at her that showed just how uncomfortable he was with her attire. He and I made eye contact. I shrugged my shoulders to indicate that I didn't know what that was all about. He gave me a weak smile back as if he was saying not to worry about it, and then he winked and got up to pour himself another drink. I watched as he threw a shot of Grey Goose back, wishing I was the one on the tip of his lips.

****

There was so much built up sexual tension between Q and me by the last night of our trip that you could feel, smell, and taste it in the air. That night, we decided to hit up a party at Mansion to see the rapper Shawty Lo perform. I danced with Q all night just to give him a preview of what I planned on putting on him later. After the club had let out, we stopped at the Waffle House to get some food. It was packed as shit, but I was digging the atmosphere, so I had no complaints. We didn't make it back to Q's crib until 5 AM. Toya passed out into a drunken coma on the couch as soon as we got inside. I took this as my chance to finally see what was up with Q without his cousin cock blocking and trying to steal the attention. I tiptoed out of the guest room and knocked on Q's door.

"Who is it?" His sexy voice alone had me ready to drop my drawers.

"It's me, V. Can I come in?"

"Yeah."

I opened his door and a cloud of smoke instantly smacked me in my face. I started coughing. Smoking was never really my thing; I was more of a drinker. Q chuckled as I tried to look cute while coughing my lungs out. When I finally regained my composure, I closed his door and slowly walked over to his bed where he was holding his blunt with one hand and playing on his PlayStation with the other.

Without saying a word, I grabbed his blunt out of his hand, took a pull and then blew it out as I laid the remainder of the blunt in the ashtray on his nightstand. He stared at me, eyes heavy and low, waiting to see what I was going to do next. I crawled onto the bed and straddled his lap, blocking his view of the TV. I closed my eyes and placed my lips on his, sliding my tongue into his mouth and then biting on his bottom lip. Kissing was never really my thing either, but from him, I wanted it all.

We kissed hungrily as he began to rub my thumping pearl through my boy shorts. Even though I could feel him growing hard as a rock under me, he still seemed a little hesitant, so I slowly grinded on him to let him know that I was OK with what was going down. I was definitely a little thrown off by how inexperienced he was acting, but it was all good. If I had to be the one to lead the way, that was fine by me. Either way, I would get mine. I stopped kissing him and lifted his shirt over his head and then took off mine.

"Where your condoms at?" I whispered in his ear between moans. He pointed to his nightstand. I reached over and grabbed a Trojan and handed it to him to put on. While he was sliding the condom on, I stood up to remove my boy shorts. I glanced over and as I expected, Q was packing and I couldn't wait to see what he felt like inside of me. I straddled his lap again and slowly slid down onto his dick. It had been a while, so I knew I had to take my time and get used to his size, but once I did it was a wrap! I rode him forward, backward, and sideways until he couldn't take it anymore and exploded in the condom. I chuckled.

"You aight?" I asked, getting up to find my boy shorts on the floor.

"Oh, you think it's funny," he said, removing the condom, huffing and puffing.

"Yeah, a little bit," I smirked. I reached for my boy shorts at the edge of the bed, but before I could get them on, Q pushed me up against his bed, bent me over and rammed his dick back inside of me.

"My turn," he whispered in my ear. Then he proceeded to fuck the smirk off my face the remainder of the night. Q had me climbing walls and screaming scriptures. As loud as I was, I couldn't believe that I hadn't woken up Toya. After three rounds, I couldn't take anymore. I tapped out and frowned as Q got the last laugh. I started to get up and head back to the guestroom to get a few z's, but to my surprise, he pulled me into him and we cuddled like we had known each other for years. *I like the way this feels,* I thought as I dozed off into La-la Land.

Chapter 12

All it took was some bomb ass sex and a lot of attention for Q to have me all in love again. We talked on the phone and texted all day every day from the time Toya and I got back to Boston. He was so sweet to me. Day by day, he melted the ice that the dudes before him had created around my heart. It was just something about him that was different from the rest. Although he hustled and was in the streets every day, he had an innocence to him that made me fall in love with him.

Da_Guy_Q88: Hey beautiful. Gud Morning. I kno u prolly still sleep but I woke up wit u on my mind like always. Have a gud day at skool today aight. And rememba shawty, the world is urs. 143

I woke up to instant messages like this almost every morning from Q and today was no different. He sent me that message at 5:15 AM. He was always up bright and early, getting to the money and he always made sure to hit me up and tell me to have a good day at school. Like they say, it's the little things that count and unlike most dudes his age, Q actually understood that saying. At this point, I was starting to think that he was too good to be true.

Vee_2xcluzive: If the world is mine I wanna be yours ☺ I'll call you between my classes xoxoxo

✳✳

After only two months of talking, we decided to make things between us official. The connection we had was undeniable. Even the thousand miles between us couldn't interfere with that. Q was supportive of every aspect of my life. From doing good in school to being a good mother to Aaliyah, he always pushed me to do better, aim higher, and he always had my back mentally.

"I'm scared, babe. What if I fail? You know I can't park for shit." I was on my way to take my road test to get my license and although I did fairly well during driving school, I was nervous beyond words.

"Aye shawty, what I tell you about doubting yourself, huh? You and I both know you got this. And if for some reason you don't pass, I'ma come up there and fuck everybody up!" I died laughing. Q always knew just what to say to make me laugh. For a moment, I forgot that I was even nervous.

"Nah, but for real, you gon' be aight, shawty. Just breathe, focus, and think about that sexy ass red BMW I'ma buy you one day. Call me after you pass so we can celebrate, aight? Love you, baby girl."

"I love you too, baby." And just like that, I passed my road test.

* *

A few weeks after making things official, I went back to Atlanta to visit him for a weekend and it was amazing. When it was time for me to fly back to Boston, I cried like a big baby. Q was my prince charming and I wanted him around every single day, not just every few months. That wasn't enough for me or for him.

"I'm going to see Q again this weekend," I told my mother over dinner.

"And who do you think is watching Aaliyah this time because I'm most definitely not. I ain't babysitting again for you to be skipping town, chasing behind some little boy." I rolled my eyes.

"Nobody was gonna ask you to watch her in the first place. She's going with Toya." I was glad I had already made arrangements so that she couldn't rain on my parade.

"No, she's not." I looked at her like she was crazy.

"Yes, she is," I said matter-of-factly. "She's my daughter and I say where she goes, not you."

"Yeah, well, y'all live in my house and I said she's not. She doesn't need to be over Toya's wild ass house. So, either find a different sitter or sit yo' hot ass still. You might be eighteen, but you still live under my roof. Remember that." This was the type of shit that I was tired of dealing with when it came to my mother. She wouldn't even allow me to make decisions and be a mother to my own child and I was sick of it.

So, I decided to move to Atlanta. I knew everyone was going to think I had lost my damn mind, so I kept it to myself while I did the necessary footwork. Of course, I had to run the idea by Q to see how he felt and he was more than down for it. He said he was excited that I was willing to take such a big step for the sake of our relationship and he couldn't wait for Aaliyah and me to get down there. Once I got the okay from my boo, the transition began. I applied to colleges. I applied for a vacant two-bedroom apartment in the same complex that Q currently lived in and then I started quoting moving trucks and budgeting my money, all with the help of Q. Once I had everything all priced and figured out, I decided it was time to finally tell my mother.

"Victoria, what the hell are you talking about?" she asked with her arms folded across her chest.

"Like I just said, Ma, me and Aaliyah are moving to Atlanta next month. That's why I keep getting all that mail from the colleges down there that I applied to." I figured if I made my sudden urge to move about school and not Q, I might have a better chance at gaining my mother's support. I knew me moving with Aaliyah wasn't going to be easy news for her to hear or accept. I was her only child and Aaliyah was her first and only grandchild. She really had no one else but us. But nothing that she could say was going to change my mind or my plans. The move was already in motion.

"Are you sure this totally unexpected move isn't about that little light skin boy that you claim to be oh so in love with?" she asked, rolling her eyes. She had met Q for the first time a few weeks ago when he came to town to visit his family for Thanksgiving. When I asked her what she thought of him, she said he was very respectable and seemed like a nice kid, but I knew damn well that didn't mean she wanted her only child moving miles away to be with him.

"No, Ma, this isn't about Q. We're not even that serious right now. This is about me wanting to pursue my dreams of becoming an interior designer. I can't do that in Boston. The industry is wack here. Atlanta is gonna open so many more doors for me, so please just try and be supportive, okay?" I begged. She shook her head.

"Okay. You're eighteen years old, V, so even if I wanted to stop you, I can't. But what I will say is that I hope that you are not up and moving my grandchild to another state to be up some little boy's ass that you barely even know. Most of these boys only want one thing. I thought you would've learned that by now, but if you haven't, you will eventually."

"And I'm hoping that eventually, you will have some faith in me instead of always assuming the worse of me. I mean I know

I'm not perfect and I've made some mistakes, but I love Aaliyah too, Ma. You're not the only one who wants what's best for her. Do I need to remind you that she is MY daughter?" I regretted those words as soon as they left my mouth. I knew how much Aaliyah meant to my mother. She didn't even respond to me. Instead, she turned and walked away with tears in her eyes. I hung my head low and dropped a few tears as well. Even though all we did was argue, I hated to see my mother sad because of me.

****

A month later, Aaliyah and I were boarding a one-way flight to Atlanta. I still couldn't believe I was about to do this, but it was too late to turn back now. My mother and Toya drove us to the airport. When it was time for us to board our flight, I expected my mother to act super dramatic, but instead, it was Toya.

"V, please don't do this. You're my best and only friend. How am I gonna live without you?" she cried hysterically. I was a little shocked that she was taking it so hard. I mean she and I were really close, but damn. She was acting like I was about to move out of the country, not the state.

"Tee, you don't have to live without me, crazy. I'm only gonna be a two-hour flight away and you know you can come visit me whenever, so please stop. I don't want to get all emotional before I get on this plane, girl, so cut the shit, okay?" I tried to lighten up the moment, but it didn't work. She just kept crying and pulling me into her, telling me not to go.

"I'm serious, V. Please don't leave me. Why are you doing this? What about us?" I was a little caught off guard by the way she was acting. Toya was never the emotional type; that was more my thing than hers. But for some reason, me moving had her in a messed up space. It was weird. Eventually, my mother grabbed hold of her so that Aaliyah and I wouldn't miss our flight. As I walked through the checkpoint with Aaliyah on my hip, I dropped a single tear for my friend who I had clearly hurt so badly with my decision.

Q picked us up from the airport and took us to his apartment. That's where we would be staying until the moving truck came with all our stuff. Aaliyah had been crying for my mother from the time we got off the plane and she still hadn't stopped once we arrived at his crib. It was like she knew something was wrong. Eventually, she cried herself to sleep. I had never seen my baby so upset for so long. It bothered me. I couldn't help but wonder if I had made the right decision leaving Boston.

✳✳

2008

One Month Later

Everything seemed to be falling into place. My apartment was slowly but surely coming together. My car had finally arrived from Boston. I had started my interior design classes and enrolled Aaliyah into a home daycare not too far from my complex. I even managed to get a little part time job a few minutes away from my school. But most importantly, Q and I were growing closer and closer every day. Even Aaliyah loved him and he definitely loved her back. She could do no wrong in his eyes.

"Aaliyah, I'm gonna spank yo' little ass if you keep telling me no, girl!" No had become her new favorite word lately.

"And if you touch her, I'm gonna spank yo' ass later tonight. You better leave my princess alone, shawty. She's a big ole meanie head, huh, lil mama?" Q said, putting Aaliyah up on his shoulders. I loved the bond they were building. Especially since I hadn't heard from Rich once since we moved. I couldn't say I was surprised, though. He didn't even have shit to say when I told him we were moving. Deadbeat ass nigga.

"Hey, bae, I just put Aaliyah down for a nap and Toya just called my cell 'cause you weren't answering yours. She said she wanna come down in a few weeks for her birthday. I told her to go on ahead and book her flight. I'm sure y'all miss each other like crazy," Q said, plopping down on the couch next to me. He placed my bare feet on his lap and began massaging them.

"Yes! That's wassup. I miss her crazy ass so much; you have no idea. It sucks having no one other than you down here to talk to. No offense, baby," I chuckled.

"None taken, shawty. I understand completely. Shit, I be missing my folks too and I've been down here a few years now on my own. Y'all two were inseparable back in the Bean, so I can only imagine how you feeling. Check this, though, when she gets here, I'll watch Aaliyah for you so y'all can hang out or whatever in peace, aight?" This is why I loved this man so much. He always tried to do whatever he could to make me happy. I didn't even respond to what he had just proposed. Instead, I took my foot out of his hand, straddled his legs, pulled out his dick and proceeded to show him just how much I appreciated him using my mouth. Who says us youngins don't know the way to a man's heart?

Chapter 13

A few weeks flew by and before I knew it, we were picking Toya up from the airport. I couldn't wait to see her crazy ass. I missed her so much since I left Boston. Although we had only been friends for four years, we had already been through so much together. Some good, some bad, but we always remained friends through it all. Plus, if it weren't for Toya, I would have never met Q, so I was extra grateful for our friendship now.

"Hey, bitch! It took y'all asses long enough to get here! Y'all were probably fucking!" she yelled, rolling her eyes as I walked towards her.

"Girl, if you don't shut your loud ass up!" I responded, embracing her. After hugging for a few seconds, we walked towards the terminal exit where Q was parked. I led the way, trying my hardest to remember which door I came in. Out of nowhere, Toya slapped me on my ass.

"Damn girl! Either you been eating good down here or Q been tearing that shit up from the back!" I fell out laughing. Toya had no filter and that's what I loved most about her. I looked at her with a devilish grin and said, "A little bit of both." We high-fived one another and continued to the car.

✳✳✳

Having Toya in Atlanta had me feeling refreshed. Not that I wasn't happy in my new living situation, but recently, I had started feeling kind of lonely and homesick. Having my best friend in town pushed all those feelings right out of the window. While she was there, we did everything from shopping to eating to sightseeing. We had to make the best of this visit because there was no telling when she would be back again. Toya insisted that we hit up the strip club, Magic City, on the last night that she was in town. It was pouring rain out and I hated the rain, but I agreed to it anyway. Nobody likes a party pooper, right?

But first I had to convince Q to let me go. We wouldn't even be able to go if he didn't agree because we needed his friend who did security to let our underage asses in. At first, he wasn't feeling it, but after I had given him some of that super head, he was on board; no questions asked. After that was settled, I went to my closet to find something to wear. I decided to wear red sequin shorts, a sheer black shirt from Express, and my black Steve Madden knee high boots. I wore diamond accessories and threw my natural hair up into a messy bun to finish my look.

"Oh, so that's how we doing it tonight, huh?" Q said sarcastically, rolling a blunt and intently watching me get dressed at the same time.

"Oh, boy! Don't start, Quincy. It's not like I have many going out clothes to choose from, so yeah, I guess this is how we doing it tonight. BUT, you and I both know who I'll be doing when I get home later tonight," I said, winking at him and licking my lips.

"Ummhmm. Just make sure y'all have y'all asses back in this spot before sunrise. Don't make me and my princess Aaliyah come looking for yall's hot asses, ya heard?" He slapped my jiggly ass.

"Yeah, daddy, I hear you," I said, planting a sloppy wet kiss right on his lips. "Now let me go do my makeup before you change yo' mind about letting me go," I playfully teased, sticking my tongue out at him as I walked out of our bedroom.

****

On the ride to Magic City, Toya and I blasted the music, swerving down the highway. I was so turnt up about my best friend being in town. I couldn't wait to get to the club and act up like we used to do in Boston. It had been too long since I had a fun night out. This was just what I needed. Just as Lil Wayne's song "Got Money" came on, Toya turned down the radio.

"Uh-uh, girl! That's my shit! Don't be touching my radio!" I playfully slapped her hand away.

"Bitch, hush. Every song is yo' damn song, let you tell it. But anyway, I have a confession to make." I looked over to see her smirking with a devilish grin.

"Oh boy, what the hell you done did now?" There was no telling with Toya's wild ass.

"Well, it's not really what I did, more like WHO I did." She chuckled at her own joke.

"Ohhhhh, do tell!" Now my curiosity was piqued.

"OK. I'll tell you, but you gotta promise not to get mad, okay?" I cut my eyes at her. Now my curiosity was beyond piqued.

"Spill it."

"Fine. I fucked your cousin, Michael!" she said all in one breath.

"TOYA!!!"

"SEE! I knew you were gonna get mad! You fucking my cousin! Why can't I fuck yours? Plus, you know I always had a crush on his fine ass anyway. It was bound to happen at some point." I swear this bitch had no shame.

"Um, that's not the point. You know how cool I am with his girl! She's damn near family to me! Why would you put me in an awkward ass position like that where I have to keep this from her?" I sucked my teeth. I was pissed. Michael's girl, Trina, had been around since I was pregnant with Aaliyah. We had grown close over the past year and Toya knew that. Shit, I had even tried to get all three of us to hang out a few times. Toya was dead wrong for this one.

"Look, girl. It only happened once and it ain't gonna happen again, so relax. I got a new boo now anyway. I ain't thinking about Michael's ass and Trina will be okay. What she doesn't know won't hurt her." I shook my head. Toya was my best friend and Michael was blood, so I wasn't going to tell Trina, but I damn sure couldn't wait to call Michael's ass tomorrow and rash on him.

****

Magic City was live as hell. Everybody was dressed to kill and the music was bumping. There were even a few celebrities in the building, making it rain. Toya and I chilled in VIP at our table, throwing back shots of Grey Goose and taking in the scenery around us. This was my first time ever being at a strip club. I hoped I wasn't making that obvious by the way I was staring with astonishment and awe all over my face. I was looking all around instead enjoying myself like everyone else was doing.

"Some of these bitches in here are bad as hell, girl. I can't even stop staring," Toya said, throwing back her third shot. She was on a roll tonight and I knew in no time her ass would be drunk as a skunk and acting up. I just hoped she was able to walk to the car because there was no way I could get her big ass there on my own.

"Yeah, some of them are definitely mad talented. Shit, I wish I could do half of the tricks that I saw up in here tonight.

Then I would really have Q's ass wrapped around my finger," I chuckled. *No wonder niggas be going broke in here,* I thought to myself.

"Girl, I ain't talking about no damn tricks! I'm talking about their bodies. Shit, I'm about to get me a lap dance from that one right over there. She's bad as fuck!" She motioned for a tatted up yellow bone chick with a fat ass and green eyes to come over to our table.

"Aye, lil mama, you checking for me?" Yellow Bone purred, licking her lips at Toya.

"Yeah, I am. Can I get a dance, boo?" Toya responded, licking her lips right back. She pulled out a fifty-dollar bill and placed it in the front of Yellow Bone's hot pink thong. I scooted over on the couch; that way, it was obvious that I wanted nothing to do with this so-called dance Toya was about to get. Yellow Bone straddled Toya frontward and began to grind on her to the music. The more she got into it, the more uncomfortable I was starting to feel. I guess it was obvious because as she was dancing, Yellow Bone looked over at me and smiled and winked, trying to ease some of my uneasiness. No luck.

Toya had always been a little touchy feely when it came to females, but to me, it seemed like she was that way with everyone, even me. I never suspected that she might actually be into females until right now. The way she and ole girl were grinding on one another had me throwing back shots left and right. That was all I could do to keep from getting up and walking away from what I was currently watching go down. When the song was finally over, I sighed in relief. I looked over just in time to see Toya and Yellow Bone kissing. Not just a peck on the lips either; these bitches were swapping spit and everything. All I could do was stare with my mouth wide open.

Once yellow bone got up and walked away to go make the rest of her money for the night, I took out my phone, trying my hardest to avoid eye contact with Toya. I knew that she could tell that I wasn't acting the same as before the dance, but I didn't know how to hide how uncomfortable I was feeling. I looked at the time and it was only 2 AM. But, after what I had just witnessed, I was ready to call it a night early and I was hoping like hell that Toya was too. I needed to get home to my man.

Chapter 14

The ride home from Magic City was a quiet one. Usually, we'd be hitting up the Waffle House for some grub and to socialize with the afterhours nightlife crowd, but tonight, I told Toya that it was probably best that we go straight home. Between my mind being all over the place from her antics tonight at the club and all the shots I had taken, I was in no condition to be making detours. We pulled up to my apartment about twenty minutes later. I switched off my ignition and Toya grabbed my hand.

"Wassup with you, V? Why you all quiet and stuff? Let me find out you can't hang no more," she asked, staring at me, trying to read my emotions.

"I'm good. I'm just feeling that Grey Goose, that's all," I lied. I tried to keep my face as casual as possible. I knew if I looked even slightly bothered Toya, of all people, would be able to tell.

"Oh OK, I feel you. You know what they say, Grey Goose get you loose." She winked before opening her door and stepping out of the car. *What the fuck was that supposed to mean?* I shook it off and got out the car behind her. When I got into my apartment, I headed straight to my bedroom to check on Q and Aaliyah. To no surprise, they were both sprawled out across my queen-sized bed, leaving nothing but the edge of the bed for me to sleep on. I was too drunk to fight with either of them about moving over, so instead, I kicked off my shoes and headed to Aaliyah's room to sleep with Toya.

"Hey, Tee, you mind if I sleep in here with you tonight? Both your cousin and Yaya done took up my whole damn bed." I shook my head in annoyance.

"Nah, get yo' ass on the couch. No suh! Of course, it's fine. This is yo' house! How the hell I'ma tell you where to sleep in your own damn house? Stop playing, girl." She threw a pillow at me. I laughed.

"Yeah, you right. Well, you're probably gonna be sleep by the time I get out of the shower, so goodnight, bestie. I'll see you in the morning."

"Night, boo."

****

A long hot shower was just what I needed. While I was in there, I couldn't stop thinking about what Toya told me before the club and what I witnessed at the club. This was a new side of Toya I was seeing and I wasn't sure if I liked it. I must have stood there letting the water run down my body for at least fifteen minutes before I even began to wash up. I stepped out of the shower and almost jumped out of my skin. Toya was standing there wrapping her hair up in her headscarf while staring at me through the mirror reflection.

"Girl, you scared the shit outta me! I didn't even hear you come in."

"My bad, boo. I knocked. I thought I heard you say come in." She had finished with her hair, but she was still staring at me intently. I quickly grabbed my towel off the sink and covered myself up.

"Oh please, V! I done seen yo' ass naked plenty of times. Don't try to act all shy now," she chuckled, walking out of the bathroom. *Thank God I brought my pajamas in the bathroom with me because I don't know what the hell is up with Tee,* I thought to myself, lotioning my damp skin with cocoa butter. I slipped on one of Q's big t-shirts and some boy shorts and wrapped up my hair. When I got back to Aaliyah's room, Toya was already in bed, texting on her phone. I hit the lights and hopped in bed beside her with our backs facing one another. As soon as my head touched the pillow, it was lights out.

****

At first, I thought I was dreaming, but then it started feeling way too good to not be happening in real life. Q was going to work between my thighs with his fingers and tongue like never before. I was in shock that he would even do something like this while his cousin was sleeping right next to me, but I damn sure wasn't going to stop him. Usually, I was the risky, adventurous one, but the thrill of what he was doing had me dripping wet. It was taking everything in me not to scream out in ecstasy as he dipped his warm tongue in and out of me.

"Oh my God, Q, what are you doing to me, baby?" I moaned, gripping the sheets that lay over his head.

"HA! Q could never make yo' pussy feel like this, boo. You better believe that!" Toya responded, lifting her head from under the covers.

"WHAT THE FUCK?!" I screamed, trying to back away. She grabbed my legs.

"Shhhhhh! You're gonna wake up Q and Yaya. Just relax, V. I've been wanting to do this for a long time now. I promise you that it won't change our friendship. Just lay back and let me finish what I started." Without giving me a chance to respond or to react, she dived back under the covers and between my legs. My mind was screaming for me to push her off me. For one, I was into some wild shit, but I definitely was not a lesbian. And more importantly, she was my man's cousin for Christ sake. Blood cousin at that! But the feeling between my legs was saying otherwise.

The things she was doing to me I had never experienced with any man. My legs were shaking in pleasure as she licked and sucked in all the right places. Shit, I couldn't find the strength to push her off if I wanted to. It felt like she was sucking my soul right out of my body. Eventually, my body began to give in and I began to grind against her vibrating, moist tongue. I grabbed her head and positioned it directly on my G-spot. She held her tongue there firmly until I exploded in her mouth. I laid there in disbelief at what I had just allowed to go down. Toya stood up and wiped all my juices off her mouth and chin with the back of her hand.

"Damn boo, you just as tasty as I thought you would be. It was definitely worth the wait," she said, walking out of the room towards the bathroom with a sly grin. Once she was out of the room, I got up to get a rag out of the linen closet so that I could clean myself up. On the way, I walked past my bedroom and a wave of guilt rushed over me. I looked at Q sound asleep with a snoring Aaliyah now lying on his chest. Right at that moment, I knew I had fucked up. It had all happened so fast. In my defense, I did think that it was Q at first. But even when I realized it wasn't him, I didn't stop her and that was the issue. I shook my head and told myself that what was done, was done and there was nothing I could do to change that now. All I could hope was that this night never came back to bite me in the ass. This was one secret that I planned on taking to the grave with me. I grabbed a blanket and went and laid on my couch. There was no way I was sleeping with Toya's freaky ass.

****

The next morning when Toya stepped out of the car, said her goodbyes, and walked into the airport, I let out a huge sigh of relief. For now, I had managed to dodge yet another bullet in my drama-filled life. When we all woke up this morning, Toya was her regular silly, loud self. She acted like absolutely nothing out of the ordinary happened last night, so I did the same, even though I could barely look her or Q in the face. I knew that any moment she could decide to spill the beans and destroy my whole relationship. But, she didn't and I was thankful. But I was even more thankful that her ass was boarding a plane back to Boston right now. Now things could go back to normal and I could also pretend like last night didn't happen.

"Damn, Tee just walked away to go back home and you already over there sighing, all sad and shit. Y'all crazy as hell, I swear. Acting like y'all can't live without each other and shit," Q said jokingly. *If only he knew the real reason my ass was over here sighing,* I thought to myself. Last night's events keep playing over and over in my head and the more I tried to ignore it, the worse I felt. I was silently praying my guilt wasn't plastered all over my face because if it was, Q would definitely read it. He just knew me like that.

While I was sitting in the passenger's seat, all in my feelings, Q was swerving through the streets of Atlanta, bobbing his head to his Lil Wayne's mixtape. He was in an extra good mood for some strange reason; the irony. I looked over at his handsome face as he drove back into town to take Aaliyah and me to brunch. He was such a beautiful sight to see and he didn't even know it. That's what amazed me about him. He was so humble and not conceited or vain at all; the opposite of myself.

"You OK, bae?" He snapped me out of my thoughts.

"Yeah, I'm okay. I love you." He smiled.

"I love yo' fine ass too."

After brunch, we took Aaliyah to the park, went to the mall, and then went and had ice cream; all at Q's expense. The more he did, the more I felt like shit. I thought about confessing what had happened last night to him over one hundred times throughout the day, but I just couldn't. I knew Q loved me, but what I did was some unforgivable shit. I might as well have fucked his brother or one of his boys; well, at least that's the way I saw it. I knew if the shoe were on the other foot, it would be a wrap for him. Knowing that alone made me keep my mouth shut. Now all I could do is hope that Toya would keep hers shut too.

Chapter 15

That night, while we were sitting on the couch together, eating dinner and watching a movie, I decided it would be a good time to bring up the idea of Q falling back from the streets some and possibly even getting a real job. This was something I had been thinking about for the past few weeks. It seemed like as our relationship was blossoming, our bills were building. Hustling was cool, but we needed steady income in our household and not just my part time job.

"Bae, I've been thinking; have you ever thought about getting a real job and only hustling on the side? That way, you're kinda doubling your money." I tried to sound as nonchalant, yet convincing as possible.

"A real job? What you mean, like a nine to five or something?" The look on his face told me that he already wasn't feeling where this conversation was heading. I figured the mention of doubling his money would distract him from what I was really trying to say, but Q was far from a dummy. He knew exactly what I was getting at. Even still, I tried to downplay things as best as I could.

"I mean, yeah, or maybe even something that's just part time; that way, you still have plenty of time to do yo' thing in the streets."

Silence.

"Don't get me wrong, baby, I respect your hustle one hundred percent, but you gotta family now. It ain't just you you gotta feed like it used to be and our bills are starting to pile up. I would take on more hours at work, but that means I would either have to drop a class or just drop out this semester altogether and that ain't even an option. I'm not tryna pressure you or anything like that. I'm just throwing the idea your way, okay?" I smiled and stroked the side of his smooth face with my finger. He looked like he was in deep thought.

"Please don't get all mad at me, Q. I'm not tryna come at you, babe; I swear to God I'm not." I wish I would have just left well enough alone. The last thing I need right now was for Q to be mad at me. I already felt fucked up as is because of last night. I sat there staring at him, hoping he wasn't going to give me the silent treatment for the remainder of the night. After a few minutes of silence, he finally spoke.

"You know what's so funny? I've actually been looking for jobs all weekend while you and Tee were out doing yall's thing. I even filled out a few applications online and shit, but I wasn't gonna say anything to you until I got offered an interview. I know we got bills that need to be paid and I know you been tryna hold it down when I can't and appreciate that shit more than you'll ever know, shawty. But honestly, you and Aaliyah make me wanna be and do better. I ain't tryna be in these streets forever. Y'all deserve better than that and I plan to give it to y'all." I swear I loved this man with all of me. He never ever ceased to amaze me with the things he said or did. It was like we just clicked, even down to our thoughts and ideas. I moved his empty dinner plate off his lap, placed it on the coffee table, and straddled his lap.

"I love you so much, Q. What would I do without you, bae?" I stared deeply into his sleepy eyes. He smiled at me, showing off those deep dimples that I loved so much. Every time he smiled, it got my panties wet instantly.

"Nothing, shawty. Wanna know why? 'Cause I ain't going nowhere and neither are you." He winked and I blushed. It was crazy how months later, he still gave me butterflies like when we first met. But the more I stared at him, those butterflies were quickly being replaced with a purring kitty. I silently thanked God that Aaliyah went down for bed early tonight because Q definitely had me ready to make up for the mistake I made last night without him even knowing I made one. I slid my tongue into his warm mouth and began kissing him passionately. He kissed me back hungrily and gripped my ass cheeks that were hanging out of my too small pajama shorts. I slid my hand into his basketball shorts and began caressing the one thing that I was craving more than anything right now.

"Go in the room and get undressed. I'll be in there in a minute." He didn't even respond. Instead, he lifted me off his lap, fixed his man in his pants and headed to our bedroom like a good little boy. He already knew what time it was. Nothing else needed to be said. I went into the kitchen to dispose of our dinner plates and pour us both a cup of Cîroc on ice, no chaser. I knew I was going to regret tonight's activities tomorrow morning when I had to drag myself to my 8 AM class, but fuck it, YOLO.

When I got to the bedroom, Q was laying in bed with nothing on but his boxers, rolling up a blunt. The only light in the room came from *American Gangster* playing on the TV screen for the hundredth time.

"You and this damn movie." I sucked my teeth. "I made you a drink, bae. And hurry up with that blunt. I gotta surprise for you." I was grinning from ear to ear like the Cheshire cat. Tonight, I wanted to be adventurous with Q. I wanted to spice things up a little bit. He deserved it. Just for simply being him and making me smile like no other man ever had. He deserved it because he had healed all my wounds from previous relationships in such a short amount of time. He deserved it because he was great to Aaliyah and was the only father figure that she ever really knew. Q was perfect to me and tonight I wanted him to feel it.

"A surprise, huh? Fuck this blunt. Come show Daddy what you got for me." He tossed his blunt onto the nightstand so fast that

I couldn't help but laugh. He was so damn silly sometimes I couldn't stand it. I stared at him staring back at me for a few seconds and then I finally spoke.

"Do you trust me, bae?" I asked innocently.

"With my life. Why, wassup?" I made a mental note of the fact that there was no hesitation in his answer. That meant that he didn't have to second-guess where my loyalty was. The feeling was definitely mutual.

"OK, well then, let me blindfold and handcuff you tonight." I waited for him to tell my ass "HELL NAH" in his aggy southern accent, but to my surprise, he simply said, "Aight." Before he could change his mind, I grabbed my furry, red handcuffs and red blindfold out of my nightstand and got him all set up for what I had in store for him.

"Where did you even get this shit from, yo'?"

"Me and Tee went to the toy store yesterday while we were out. Now, no more questions, aggy." I stripped down to my satin bra and thong set I had on under my pajamas so that I would be nice and comfortable while pleasing my man.

"V, what the hell are you doing, girl? Why is it so quiet and shit? You better not be 'bout to do no dumb shit. Word up." I could hear the nervousness in his voice.

"Relax, baby. I'm right here. I was just getting comfortable. I wouldn't even play you like that. I thought you said you trust me," I said sarcastically.

"I do, but still. I know how you like to play sometimes." I wanted to laugh because I could tell that he was getting pissed off, but instead, I took a sip of my drink while massaging his already semi-hard manhood. In no time, it was rock hard and ready, so I lowered my mouth onto it and waited for him to react to the cold ice that was still in my mouth. At first, he tensed up, but as I continued to bob my head up and down his shaft the ice began to melt, my mouth got warmer and wetter and his toes began to curl.

"Damn girl, you on some other shit tonight, huh?" he said, biting down on his bottom lip. "I swear to God when you let my hands free, I'ma pound that pussy till it's numb." I smirked while flicking my tongue across the tip of his dick. "Yeah, yeah, we'll see. Wait right here. Well, actually, you don't really have a choice, now do you?" I chuckled at my own joke while walking out of the bedroom towards the kitchen.

A few minutes later, I returned to the room with all my ingredients. The remainder of the night, I sucked every topping I could find in my kitchen off every inch of Q's body until he was insisting that I let his hands free and take the blindfold off. But I wouldn't give in. I needed to show him just how much he meant to me. I needed him to know that even though I fucked up last night and he didn't know it, I never would again. I needed him to know that he was all I needed and I was all he needed too.

I gave him all of me that night and when I finally did let his hands free, he wasted no time repaying me for all that I had just done to him. He devoured my pussy for what seemed like hours and then fucked me into a coma. My whole body was sore when he was done with me. I was so weak I couldn't even find the energy to get up and shower. I knew Q would be clowning me the next day and I damn sure wasn't making it to my first class, but I didn't even care. Tonight was well worth it. They say true love is hard to find and based on my past, I would usually be the first one to believe them. But after tonight, that was no longer the case. I fell asleep with a big smile plastered on my face thinking, *this has to be what real love is all about. Damn, I'm lucky as hell. I'd have to be the stupidest female ever to fuck this up. I will never find another man who loves me like he does. I finally found my happily ever after. Thank you, God.*

Chapter 16

The next day while I was out grocery shopping for the house, I got a call out of the blue from Rochelle. We hadn't been keeping in contact as much as we used to. Now that I was over Rich and no longer cared who he was or wasn't fucking, I didn't have much use for our "friendship". Even still, it was nice to hear from someone back home other than my immediate family and Toya. So, when she asked if she could come stay with me in a few days, I said yes, even though it was such short notice; my gut told me not to agree. She gave me some sob story about how she was thinking about transferring to a historically black college next year and her first choice was Clark Atlanta. She had bought a flight and was stay with her cousin, but her cousin reneged, so now she needed somewhere to stay while she was in town, touring the school. I was hesitant to have her around Q, but I knew she wasn't crazy enough to try nothing stupid, so I agreed.

I picked her up from the airport that Friday night and the first thing she asked me when she got in the car was where we were partying that night. *I see some shit never changes,* I thought to myself, shaking my head.

"We can go to this lil spot near my crib, but we can't be out all night. My boo doesn't play that shit. He wants me right there next to him when he goes to sleep for the night." I rubbed it in her face purposely.

"Awwww, that's mad sweet. I'm happy for you, girl." She was so fake it was ridiculous. I played along, though.

"Thanks, girl. What's been up with you, though? I haven't heard from you in a while." I was swerving in and out of the Atlantic traffic trying to hurry back so Q could get a few more hours in the trap before I asked him to babysit Aaliyah so I could go out. I knew he wouldn't mind, but I also knew that he would be missing out on money once he said yes. I always tried to be considerate of things like that; we were a team.

"Nothing much. Just going to school and work, and partying, of course. You know that ain't never gonna change." We both laughed. Her, because she thought that what she said was funny, and me, because I thought that what she had just said was sad as fuck. To each his or her own, though.

"Yeah, I know. Partying will forever be the center of your life. But damn, yo' boo don't make you sit yo' ass down sometimes?" I couldn't wait to hear her response to this one.

"I don't have a boo, girl. I'm single." And I knew why, but for now, I kept that to myself.

"Damn, no boo at all? You lying." I played it off like I didn't already know what was up.

"Nope. I'm serious. I'm all set on these wack ass Boston dudes. Rich fucked it up for everybody." I laughed out loud. She laughed too. Little did she know I was laughing at her and not with her, yet again. Just a week or two ago, Toya had called me telling me how a friend of hers went to school with Rochelle and their dorm room was on the same floor. She said she was coming out of her room a few times and saw Rich going in and out of Rochelle's room. That meant Rochelle was fucking with Rich again now that I had moved away. Sneaky little bitch. Or should I say, scary little bitch.

"Oh, yeah? You still tripping off that shit with Rich? I've been over his ass." Now I was just entertaining myself. Fuck it.

"I've been over him too. I'm just saying." she lied. And she did it with a straight face.

"Yeah, I feel you. When is the last time you spoke to him anyway?" I already knew the answer, but I wanted to see what lie she would come up with this time. Her hesitation told me she was thinking of the right answer.

"Girl, it's been so long I couldn't tell you. I don't have a reason to talk to him after what he put me through. That nigga is a liar and a cheater. Oh, and a user too. Let's not forget that one. I'm all set on his ass." I had to hold back my laughter as I let her continue to make a fool of herself, bashing a nigga that she was still fucking with. The shit was plain ole sad.

"I honestly feel bad for you 'cause you have a kid with him, so you have to be in contact with him for yall's daughter's sake." I shook my head. The nerve of this bitch. She felt bad for me, yet she was the one still fucking him. I was confused. If anything, she should've been feeling bad for herself. She clearly had no self-respect or dignity.

"Nah, don't feel bad for me. I haven't even spoken to Rich since I told him I was moving. That was months ago. He doesn't give a shit about Aaliyah, so I don't give a shit about him. I will NEVER give that nigga the time of day again." I emphasized the word never purposely just to fuck with her. Nevertheless, unlike her, I was speaking the truth.

"Yeah, I feel you. Me either. He definitely missed out fucking us over. Fuck him, though." I was dying on the inside at the irony of what she just said. I drove the rest of the way in silence. I couldn't wait for this weekend to be over so I could send this clown back to Boston where she came from.

****

The whole time Rochelle was at my house, I kept a close eye on her and made sure that she was never left alone with Q. Luckily for me, he was hardly home, so their interaction was limited anyway. I didn't want to have to kill Rochelle's ass for real this time. She could have Rich, but Q was off limits. I would go to jail over him with no problem. I never told Q the truth about how me and Rochelle became "friends" in the first place, so he never suspected a thing when she first got there. Q didn't know that side of me because he never gave me a reason to act that way. As long as he continued to behave, he would have no reason to ever see my crazy side.

On her last day in town, we all got up and went to Lennox Mall. Everything was cool until I noticed Rochelle being a little too friendly while we were all having lunch at the food court. I didn't want to alarm Q, so I waited until he got up to make a phone call to pull her up on it.

"Damn Rochelle, you acting like you've known my man for years." I said it in a joking manner, but I damn sure wasn't joking. I knew that she would catch my drift. She quickly started to explain and make excuses.

"Not even. He just reminds me of my older brother a lot. What did you say his sign was again?" She tried to play it off.

"I never told you what his sign was. I never told you anything about him except his name and that he's mine." I'm sure she could tell by the tone of my voice where I was going with this.

"Oh. Well, yeah, that's all it is. I'll chill out, though. I don't want any problems." *I bet her scary ass doesn't.*

"Yeah, thanks. I don't want you to have any problems either."

And just like that, Rochelle was pretty much quiet until we dropped her off at the airport that evening. I walked her inside to help her with her bags. When we got to her terminal, we embraced in a fake ass hug and said our goodbyes. She promised to come back soon to visit, but I knew that wasn't happening. I was sure that the next time I would end up catching a murder charge if she even breathed at Q the wrong way. She could stay her ass right in Boston with Rich's lame ass. I didn't need her sneaky ass sniffing around my future husband.

I walked back to the car and hopped in. Q was sitting there with a weird expression on his face.

"Wassup, bae?" I asked. He seemed fine on the drive to the airport.

"That girl is not yo' friend, V." I smiled. My baby knew what was up.

****

Later on that night, my curiosity got the best of me. Q and I were laid up watching *Dora the Explorer* with Aaliyah when I decided to find out why he had said what he said earlier.

"Baby, what made you say what you said about Rochelle earlier?"

"What you mean?"

"You said she's not my friend. What made you say that? You barely know her."

"Shit, shawty, I ain't gotta know her to know she wanna be you. A blind man can see that." I made a confused face. His answer had completely caught me off guard. I had always known that Rochelle was jealous of me, but I never thought of it as her wanting to be me.

"Wow, babe. I never looked at it that way."

"Well, now you know. That girl most definitely wanna be you, shawty. And shit, I can't say that I blame her 'cause you bad as fuck. Now come here." He pulled me in closer to him and planted a kiss on my forehead. Rochelle could try all she wanted, but she would never be me. And she would damn sure never have my Q. He was all mine, forever.

Chapter 17

Over the next two weeks, Q went on a few interviews, but he didn't get any calls for second interviews or job offers. With every unsuccessful interview, his frustration started to build and eventually, it started to take a major toll on our relationship. It seemed like we were arguing every day now. We hardly spent any quality time like we used to. Slowly, but surely, shit was starting to go downhill for us. Q spent the majority of his time up the street at his old apartment, which was now just a trap house and the chill spot for all his boys, and Aaliyah and I spent all our time together at home, alone.

Today, my boss decided to give me the day off with pay. She said I seemed a little off the past few days and that she could tell that I needed a "mental health day". Boy, was she right. I'm sure the stress I was feeling was written all over my face. I walked into my apartment and kicked off my six-inch Steve Madden pumps. The house was quiet, so I knew that meant Q was more than likely up the street. I had a few hours before I had to pick Aaliyah up from daycare, so I decided to make myself a sandwich, take a power nap, and then work a little on my project for school that was due next week. I opened my fridge and noticed immediately that the light inside didn't come on. I stuck my hand inside and noticed it didn't feel cold inside either. I checked the freezer. Same result.

"Hmmm, maybe I need a new fridge or something. Let me walk my ass down to the rental office and put in a maintenance request before my food starts to thaw out and go bad," I said out loud. I walked to my room to grab some flip-flops and then headed to the bathroom to wash my face before heading back out the door. I flicked the bathroom light switch and nothing happened. *What the fuck?* I tried again. Nothing. I walked all over my apartment flicking every single light switch until I finally accepted the fact that the electricity company had finally gotten tired of letting me slide with an unpaid bill and had shut off the electricity just like they said they would. I sighed and grabbed my cell phone out of my purse to call Q. He picked up on the first ring.

"Wassup?"

"The lights are off," I responded, annoyed by his dry ass greeting.

"It's daytime, why would they need to be on?" *What a dumb ass.*

"No, Quincy, the lights are SHUT off. As in the electricity company shut them off!" I couldn't believe I had to clarify this.

"Ohhhh. Damn. How that happen?" *And the stupidity continues.*

"How do you think it happened? Our bill is damn near $250. Eventually, they were gonna get tired of warning us and actually do something about it."

"True. Well, how much you gotta pay them to get it put back on?" Now we were getting somewhere.

"Well, the shut-off notice says at least half plus an extra thirty-dollar reconnection fee if they cut it off, so I would say at least $150."

"Aight. You got that?" I sucked my teeth.

"Really? Was that a serious question?" This nigga knew damn well I spent my last twenty dollars last night on pampers and wipes for Aaliyah.

"I mean, yeah, kinda. Shit's looking real slow right now on my end, so I definitely ain't got that much. I might be able to do like fifty now and another fifty later today." This was the exact shit that I was talking about. Q was supposedly out in these streets hustling every single day, yet he was forever broke. Where the fuck was all the money going?

"I'm broke until Friday, Q, but you knew that already, though. And I'm pretty sure that fifty dollars is not gonna be enough to convince these people to turn our shit back on, so we need to figure something out like right fucking now." I was starting to get frustrated. I could already tell what I was going to end up having to do; call my mother.

"Chill with all the attitude, shawty. Straight up. I'ma try to figure something out, aight?" And with that, he hung up. That shit only pissed me off even more. I threw my phone on my nightstand and got comfortable for my much-needed nap, but not before sending Q a nice little text first.

> *Thank you for hanging up in my face. Real cute. I'm 'bout to take a nap before I go get Aaliyah. Let there be light by the time I wake up or else. Toodles.*

✳✳

And of course, when I woke up one hour later, the only light was the light shining in from the windows. I called Q, ready to go off. He must've thought I was joking when I said or else.

"Yo'."

"Yo' nothing! The lights are still off. What the fuck is going on?" My patience was wearing real thin at this point.

"I only got $100 right now. You might have to call yo' moms for the rest and I'll give it back to y'all when I get it." I knew that was coming. That was exactly what I didn't want to do, but I knew that I had to. My mother was the only person I knew I could depend on at all times, hands down. Plus, there was no way I was going to have my baby girl coming home to a dark apartment. That wasn't even an option. I didn't even respond to Q. I hung up and mentally prepared myself for the phone call that I knew was about to aggravate my entire existence. I had no time to stall, though. The electricity company would be closing soon. My mother answered on the very first ring.

"Hey, baby girl! To what do I owe this midday phone call? Let me find out you miss Mommy already!" *She's so damn extra, I swear.*

"Hey, Ma, of course I miss you. How is your day going so far?"

"It's going. Today was a little hectic at work, but hey, what day isn't? Where is my baby at? I miss her so much. Can't wait to see her lil chunky butt next week." Aaliyah was turning two next week and of course, my mother took it upon herself to book a flight to Atlanta without even asking me.

"I'm actually on my way to get her right now. But I called to ask for a favor if you can do it. Something crazy is going on with my bank card, so I can't use it or take my money out until the bank opens tomorrow, but I have a bill that I have to pay by today. Do you think you can Western Union me over a few dollars and I'll give it back to you?" I felt bad for lying, but there was no way I was going to tell her what the real situation was. I would never hear the end of it.

"Yeah, no problem, mama. How much do you need? And you're gonna have to give me your account information and stuff 'cause I ain't going back out the house to no Western Union. I'm tired and I'm already in my pajamas on my couch. I will make a payment online for you." *Well, that was easy.* I pulled in front of

Aaliyah's school and read her off my account information. I told her to just put fifty dollars. When I got back home, I would get the other $100 from Q and apply it to the bill myself. I let her speak to Aaliyah briefly and then we said our goodbyes and hung up.

****

On the way home, I stopped by This Is It to grab dinner. I was in no mood to cook. I honestly just wanted to settle Aaliyah and knock out so that I didn't have to interact with Q when he decided to bring his ass home. While standing in line, trying to figure out whether I wanted baked chicken or fried chicken, someone tapped me on the shoulder. I slowly turned around, ready to curse whoever thought it was okay to touch me the fuck out. My mouth dropped when I saw who it was. There stood Jason, looking good enough to fuck right there in the restaurant.

I had met Jason about two years ago through Trina and I had been crushing on him since. He was tall and light-skinned with a muscular, yet slender build. He had braids that he always wore in perfect straight backs and full luscious lips that hid his perfect white teeth. He smiled at me and I almost came on myself.

"Just as beautiful as I remember you." I blushed.

"Look who's talking. What are you doing around these parts?" I tried not to stare too hard at his imprint showing clear as day through his gray sweatpants.

"I came to find you. Who told you you could move away on me?" His face was so serious I almost believed him. I knew better, though.

"Boy, please. What are you really doing down here?" He chuckled.

"Nah. I'm down here visiting family. I did hope that I bumped into you though and look; must be fate." I swear this nigga had game for days and I was falling for all of it. I had a little game of my own, though.

"Maybe, maybe not. Depends on what you do from here." I knew I was dead wrong for my response, considering I had a boyfriend and all, but a little flirting never hurt anybody, right?

"Oh yeah, well let me start by giving you my number again since you never used it before. And if I'm lucky enough, you'll use it this time and give me a chance to prove to you that this encounter wasn't by chance." Against my better judgment, I took his number. Again, a little flirting never hurt anyone, right?

Chapter 18

When I got back to my apartment, Q had already gone to the electricity company and gave them the $100 he came up with. I was assuming my mother had done her part online too because the lights were already back on. I thanked God for that, but of course, I still walked around the house giving Q the silent treatment for the rest of the night. I knew he was trying to do better, but honestly, at this point, trying just wasn't good enough anymore. I needed results.

I prepared dinner, fed and bathed Aaliyah, cleaned up and put her to bed all without saying one word to Q. It wasn't too hard to do since he was in and out the whole time just like every night. For somebody with no money, the boy barely stayed still. After Aaliyah was asleep, I hopped in the shower and stood there for thirty minutes or so trying to ease my mind. When I walked into my room, Q was laying there, playing on his game. I rolled my eyes and grabbed my pajamas to get dressed. I even made sure to put on underwear. There wouldn't be any funny business going on tonight. His ass was on punishment until further notice and he needed to know it.

"So you just not gonna talk to me all night?" Q asked as I climbed into bed on my side and turned my back to him.

"I ain't got shit to say," I responded with an attitude.

"Oh, yeah? That's cool. Well, it seems to me like you need some space, shawty." I sucked my teeth.

"Did I say that I needed space?"

"No, but actions speak louder than words and yo' movements all night are telling me that there's a problem. You want me to rest my head down the street for tonight?" I wanted to tell him if he did, he might as well move his ass right back down there, but I refrained. I knew that wasn't what I wanted. I was just mad right now.

"Do what you want, Quincy. I'm going to bed." I closed my eyes, hoping he wouldn't say shit else to me. My responses might not be as cordial next time around. But I was also hoping that he didn't get up to leave. If he did, it would tell me a lot about where we stood. I heard him turn the game off and flick off the lamp on his nightstand, and then I felt him wrap his arm around me and pull me into him.

"I love you," he whispered in my ear. I smiled.

"Love you too."

Just as I was about to doze off, I heard my text message notification chime; it was my mother.

I see some things still haven't changed with you, Victoria. You still like to half ass tell the truth as if I won't do my own research. I paid the remaining balance on your bill. I refuse to have my grandbaby in a house with no electricity, AGAIN. I'm not sure what the hell is going on down there, but I will definitely find out when I get there. Goodnight.

I shook my head in disbelief. *Here we go…*

****

Having my mother at the house a few days later started off as a disaster. The night before I picked her up from the airport, Aaliyah had a fever and was vomiting everything she ate out of nowhere. Q suggested that maybe she was teething, but from what I could see, she had a mouthful of teeth already. My baby was sick and right now definitely wasn't the time for her to be. When I picked my mother up, Aaliyah still wasn't feeling well, so of course, she used that as a way to start with her bullshit.

"Why is my baby in the backseat looking like she's about to pass out? Have you fed her today?" She hadn't even been in the car five minutes and she was already implying that I wasn't doing what I needed to do as a mother.

"Of course I fed her. It's 10 AM. She hasn't been feeling well since last night, so we had a very long night. She's tired." I honestly didn't even feel like I needed to explain myself about MY kid, but I was trying to avoid arguing with her as long as possible.

"Well, what's wrong with her?"

"I don't know, Ma. She had a fever and she was vomiting all last night. But now her temperature is down and she hasn't vomited yet today. She probably just ate something bad yesterday or something simple like that. She's fine."

"Hmmm, sounds like food poisoning to me. Did you feed her something that might have gone bad while sitting in your fridge the whole time your lights were off for all those hours?"

I wanted to pull over and put her ass out my car right at that moment because I already knew where this conversation was about to go, but I caught myself. If I wanted these next few days to go smoothly, I had to think first and speak after. I had to beat my mother at her own game. So, instead, I just responded, "Nah, we had take-out last night. We just won't eat from there no more." Problem solved.

When we got to my apartment, it was no different. She complimented everything and then followed up with some kind of criticism. I just ignored her and let Aaliyah enjoy her company while Q and I isolated ourselves in our bedroom. The rest of her stay wasn't too bad. We went to the malls; I showed her my job and my school. She met Aaliyah's teachers, and on Aaliyah's birthday, we had cake and ice cream. I was patiently waiting for her to bring up the electricity situation again, but she never did. On her last night there, she and I watched a movie in the living room together. Aaliyah was asleep and Q was out, like always. I had to admit that I was kind of sad she was leaving the next day. As much as she got on my nerves, I still loved her more than words could explain. When the movie was over, she looked over at me on the other couch with a weird expression.

"Why you looking at me like that?" She went from chilling to looking super serious. It was weird.

At first, she didn't say anything and then she looked me right in my eyes and said, "You and Aaliyah need to come back to Boston, Victoria."

****

The next morning, my mother and I dropped Aaliyah at school before heading to the airport so she could finally head back home. It had been a long week having her at my house, but I had to admit that I did enjoy her company. It killed me watching her and Aaliyah part ways. Even though Aaliyah loved her mommy, she was most definitely a Nana's girl from day one; there was no denying that. The conversation my mother and I had the night before kept replaying in my head. My mother had revealed so much to me while telling me why she felt like Aaliyah and I needed to come back to Boston. After listening to her, I couldn't help but start considering it. I had no clue that my mother had been in the hospital twice since my move. I guess everyone felt that it was best to keep it from me so I wouldn't be worried. I felt like it was fucked up, but hey, what could I do? According to her, she was having bad migraines, becoming lightheaded very often, and also complained of her heart racing at times. The doctors told her it was stress and anxiety and of course, she blamed the stress and anxiety on me being 1,000 miles away with her grandbaby. Go figure. We pulled up to the airport and I got out of my car to help her get her bags out the trunk.

"So, did you think about what I said to you last night, Victoria? I know you still gonna do whatever it is you wanna do, but at least think about it, please." I could hear the plea and sadness in her voice.

"OK, Ma. I heard everything that you said last night and I'm gonna think about it all. Please just don't start riding my back about it, okay?" I had enough going on lately without her pressuring me to do what she thought was best. I needed to figure out what was best on my own for once.

"I'm not riding your back. I'm just making sure you understand where I'm coming from. But I'll leave you alone about it for now. Come give me a hug so I don't miss my flight and so you can make it to class on time." I gave her a long, tight hug and promised to call her later. I watched as she walked into the airport and fought back tears as I thought about what I would do and how I would feel if something bad ever happened to her. I knew at that moment that she was right; I needed to go back home.

****

I tried my hardest to focus in my classes, but I just couldn't. I couldn't focus during my work shift either. All I could think about was my mother's well-being and how Q was going to take it when I told him I wanted to move back to Boston. Of course, I would finish out my semester of school first, but after that, I was ready to be out. I didn't know if he would be happy or mad about it, especially considering all the recent tension between us. To me, it made sense anyway. We both had family and security in Boston and we were clearly struggling where we were right now, so why stay when we had the option of leaving? The solution to our problems seemed to be sitting right in our faces the whole time. We just needed to make the first steps. I didn't know how Q would feel about starting all over as far as his street shit went, but what I did know was that I wanted him to leave with me and I would be hurt if I couldn't get him to agree to do it, but I was going back either way. My mind was already made up. With or without him, Aaliyah and I were moving back to Boston once I was done with school.

<u>Chapter 19</u>

After work, I picked Aaliyah up and headed straight home to cook and take a nice long hot shower. The stress of everything going on had my body tense and my head pounding with thoughts. Just as I was about two blocks away from my complex, I heard sirens blaring behind me. I pulled to the right of the road to let the police car by, but instead, it pulled right behind me. I immediately got nervous; I had never been pulled over in the nine months that I had been driving. I knew I wasn't speeding, I was too tired to speed, so I had no idea what the hell I could possibly be being pulled over for. I rolled down my window as the white middle-aged male officer approached.

"License and registration, please." I could tell from his tone and stance that if I had actually done something, he wasn't going to give me a warning for it. I handed him my information.

"Here you go, officer. Do you mind me asking what exactly I am being pulled over for?" I was trying to be as polite as possible. I knew from TV that all traffic stops could go one of two ways, especially down here in the south.

"Well, to be honest, young lady, I pulled you over because you don't look old enough to be driving this here vehicle. And since your plates are out of state, it's my duty to make sure this vehicle isn't stolen and that you are in fact old enough to be driving." This was some bullshit. Now, I know I still had a baby face and I still wore the same size clothes and shoes that I did when I first started high school, but really?

"Sir, I am eighteen years old. That is my two-year-old daughter sitting in the back seat. I can assure you that my license is valid and that I am old enough to be driving. In fact, I am also the

OWNER of this vehicle that I am driving." *He got me fucked up,* I thought to myself.

"Yeah, well, we'll just have to see now, won't we?" He took my information and walked back over to his car. It had to be about twenty minutes before he came back to my window. By this point, my annoyance was at a level ten and it was hard for me to hide it.

"Well, looks like everything checked out, so I'm gonna let you go with a warning, this time. But next time, you might wanna slow down a bit or else I'm gonna be forced to write you a ticket. Have a good day, ma'am." I chuckled as I rolled up my window and pulled off. First, I looked too young, then it was my plates, and now I needed to slow down. I was pretty sure that I had just experienced my first case of DWB-Driving While Black.

****

When I finally made it home, I immediately placed Aaliyah on her potty for "Potty Party Time" as we called it and hopped in the shower. I stepped out twenty minutes later and I heard my phone ringing; it was Toya's ringtone. I ran into my room to pick it up.

"Hello?"

"Damn bitch, what you in there doing? Fucking? All outta breath and shit. This is the third time I called yo' ass!" Toya was always assuming somebody was fucking because she always was.

"My bad. I was in the shower. I just got out. Wassup tho'?"

"Ohhhh, the shower, huh? So, that means you standing there all wet and naked for me?"

I had no idea how to respond to that, so I just laughed it off and said, "Girl, stop playing and tell me what's going on. You ain't call three times in a row for nothing." I was hoping like hell she would stop with the gay shit. I was still trying my hardest to forget about what happened a few weeks back between us.

"Yeah, let me stop playing with yo' scary ass. But yeah, you right. I didn't call for nothing; I called to tell you the great news. I'm pregnant, bitccchhhh!"

"Wait, what?! Pregnant? How the hell are you pregnant with no man? I am all the way lost right now! I mean, congrats, but please help me understand this." Toya hadn't had a boyfriend since who knows when. I was praying like hell she didn't slip up and get pregnant by some random nigga.

"Actually, I do have a man. Remember the dude Kevin I was telling you about when I was down there? The one I met in the club a few months back? We been kicking it ever since then. That's my baby."

"Toya, that wasn't even three whole months ago. You mean to tell me you pregnant by him already? You barely even know his ass. Like, damn bitch, do you even know the nigga's last name?" I knew Toya was wild, but this shit took the cake. She was out here acting like the same dumb bitches that we talked shit about on the regular. And furthermore, this involved a child, not just her and her reckless ways. I was disappointed in her and I couldn't even try to hide it or pretend to be happy about what she just told me.

"Girl, bye. You sound like my momma right now. Chill the fuck out. I didn't call you for all of that. Wasn't nobody talking shit or lecturing you when yo' ass got knocked up at fifteen, so save it. I am nineteen years old and damn near grown. I called thinking that my best friend would be happy for me, but I guess I was wrong." Toya was right. I had some nerve judging her situation when I was only eighteen years old and already had a two-year-old.

"You're right, Tee. I'm sorry. Congrats, girl. I can't wait to be an auntie and spoil my niece or nephew. I'm happy for you and whatever his name is. I really am."

"His name is KEVIN, bitch. Don't be funny!" We both fell out laughing. We could never stay mad at each other for long. And regardless of what happened between us while she was visiting, she was still my best friend. Something was bothering me, though, and I had to ask.

"On a serious note, though, I gotta ask you something, Tee, and please don't get offended. Are you sure that baby ain't my cousin's?" I was praying like hell she said she knew for sure that it wasn't.

"Girl, this is not Michael's baby! Get the hell out of here!" I knew Toya well and she didn't sound too sure of herself, so I decided to press the issue.

"How do you know?" She sucked her teeth.

"Um, because it's my pussy and I know, damn V!" She was starting to get mad, so I decided to let it go, for now.

"Aight. Don't get all mad, geesh."

"I'm not getting mad I just can't believe you would even ask me some dumb shit like that." I decided to try and make things better.

"I only asked 'cause I care about you, Tee. You know damn well I wasn't trying to come at you."

"Yeah, aight. So anyway, enough about me, wassup with you and Q? You ain't done with his bum ass yet?" Lately, I noticed that Toya was on some other shit when it came to Q. I had been trying to ignore it, but it seemed like every time we spoke, she always had something negative to say about her own cousin. I didn't know what the problem was, but it was starting to piss me off.

"First of all, how are you calling your own cousin a bum? And second of all, if he's such a bum, why the hell did you introduce me to him?" Technically, Q and I would've never hooked up if it wasn't for Toya.

"Cousin or no cousin, I call 'em how I see 'em and from what I can see, you the only one holding y'all down while he sitting around all day doing nothing but claiming he's a hustler. So, that makes him a what? Ding! Ding! Ding! You guessed it! A bum!" She laughed loudly at her own joke, but I didn't see shit funny. There was no way I was about to sit on the phone and bash my man and neither was she. Right as I was about to go in on her ignorant ass, my other line beeped. It was an unknown number; I ignored it.

"You not funny and you need to grow up, Toya. I don't know what yo' issue is with Q but..." My other line started ringing again. Unknown. I usually wouldn't even consider answering, but something inside of me told me to answer this time since the caller had called back to back.

"Let me call you back, that's my other line." She was so lucky that curiosity was getting the best of me at this moment. Whoever was calling had just helped her dodge a bullet for now. There would always be later, though.

"Ummmhmmm. I know that's probably Q calling to ask what you cooked for dinner after his ass did nothing all day. That's y'all, though, I guess. Anyway, tell El Broko I said wassup." I didn't even respond. I would curse her the fuck out for that later because she was out of line at this point. In the meantime, I clicked over and tried to disguise my voice just in case it was a bill collector trying to catch me slipping.

"Hello?"

"You have a collect call from Q, an inmate at the DeKalb County Detention Center. To accept this call…"

My phone hit the floor.

Chapter 20

My throat felt like it was closing and my vision started to get blurry. This shit had to be some kind of sick joke. Or maybe I just misheard the name that was said and whoever was calling from jail dialed the wrong number. *Yeah, that's exactly what it was,* I told myself as I tried to regain my composure.

No one on the corner gotta swagga like us, swagga like us, swagga swagga like us...

I knew from the ringtone coming through my phone that it was an unknown number calling back again. I picked my phone up off the floor with shaky hands and pressed the green button to answer.

"Hello?" I said faintly.

"You have a collect call from Q, an inmate at the DeKalb County Detention Center. To accept this call for a one-time charge of $9.99, please press 1. To decline this call, please press 2 or hang up."

It was Q. This was real. I recognized his voice immediately when he stated his name, so I knew for sure that it was him. I pressed 1, grabbed my wallet and got ready to enter my debit card information so that I could accept the call. I closed my eyes and waited to be connected.

"Baby?"

"What the fuck, Q?! Please tell me this is some kinda mistake! Why are you calling me from jail? This cannot be happening right now!" The tears poured down my face and I couldn't stop them, even if I tried. I felt it in my heart that whatever was going on right now wasn't going to be good news.

Silence.

"I fucked up. But I ain't tryna say too much over this phone, though. Just call up here tomorrow morning and see when my visits are. Come up here as soon as they say you can. We'll talk more then. And set up yo' phone for whenever I call you back. Everything gon' be aight, I promise."

"No, everything is not gonna be aight! Fuck waiting for a visit! You need to tell me what the hell is going on right now, Q. Like what am I even supposed to do right now?" At this point, I could feel myself hyperventilating. I had so many mixed emotions going on inside of me. How could this be happening right now? As if we weren't already going through enough bullshit.

"First, what I need you to do is stop all that crying. Like I said, we gon' be aight. Then I need you to do everything I just told you to do. Plus, I need you to call the bail bondsman in the morning too, to see what my bail is looking like. I need you to be strong and hold me down, V. Ain't no time for crying right now…"

"You have one minute remaining…"

"Look, this phone 'bout to hang up. Call my moms and let her know wassup when we hang up and do all that other stuff in the morning, aight? I love you, shawty."

"I love you too. When are you gonna call me again? How am I supposed to know that you're okay?"

"Thank you for using Securus. Goodbye."

As soon as the call disconnected, I broke down. I had never felt so scared and alone in my entire life. Q and I may not have been on the best of terms recently, but other than Aaliyah and my mother, he was all I had. I cried until I couldn't cry anymore. When I finally pulled myself together a little bit, I texted Q's mother and let her know that her son was locked up like he had asked me to. If he didn't ask me to, I wouldn't have. It wasn't like she was going to do anything but ask one million questions but offer no solution, and that's exactly what she did. Unfortunately, for both of us, I knew just as much information as she did, so I politely ended the conversation by saying I would contact her when I knew more. I climbed into Aaliyah's bed and cuddled up with her for comfort. I silently cried myself to sleep, hoping this was all just a bad dream.

✻✻

The next morning when I woke up, Q wasn't anywhere to be found in our apartment and when I called his cell phone, it kept going to voicemail. That confirmed that last night wasn't a dream. It was real life and now I had to figure out what was next. I sat Aaliyah in her high chair so she could eat her oatmeal before daycare. I called up to the jail and gave them Q's information so they could look him up and tell me when he could get a visit. Since he had already been booked and assigned a cell, they informed me that he was able to receive visits that night between 7 PM and 9 PM. I asked them what his charges were, but they weren't trying to come up off any information, so instead, I just asked for the number to the bails bondsman and hung up. Next, I called the bail bondsman and things quickly went from bad to horrible.

"What do you mean his bail is $10,000? What did he do, kill somebody?" I had never even seen that much money in my life, let alone had to pay it just to get someone out of jail. The bail bondsman chuckled.

"Ma'am, if he killed somebody, he probably wouldn't even have a bail. Ten thousand dollars isn't as bad as it sounds since you only have to pay me ten percent of that to get him out, which is only $1,000." He said only $1,000 like that shit was nothing. I mean it was much better than $10,000, but still, where the hell was I supposed to pull an extra $1,000 from when I was already struggling to pay my bills?

"Okay, and how much time do I have to give you that?"

"Take as much time as you need. The sooner you pay me, the sooner he gets out, though."

"And I have to give you the whole amount in order for him to get out?"

"That's right."

"OK, well, I don't have that much at this exact moment, but I need to get him out so what am supposed to do?"

"Call me back when you do have it." Click.

I stared at the phone in disbelief. I guess I had to come up with $1,000 or Q would be stuck in jail until who knows when. I sent his mother a quick text telling her the new information I had just found out and of course, got no response. Now that it was time to talk money, I already expected her to go MIA. Luckily, my class for the day was canceled, which meant I could go to work for a few extra hours. I dropped Aaliyah off and cried my entire drive to work. As soon as I got settled at my desk, my boss called me into her office.

"Victoria, is everything alright? No offense, but you look drained, honey. Your eyes are swollen and red and your hair is a mess, which is a rare occasion for you. Are you feeling okay?"

I wanted to tell her so badly that I wasn't okay. In fact, I was the opposite and trying my hardest at that exact moment not to fall apart. But, I didn't need her in my business, so instead, I just responded, "I'm just having some minor family issues, but I'll be fine. I'm sure being here at work will help me keep my mind off things, so I'm gonna get back to work if that's okay. Thank you for checking on me."

"Okay. Let me know if you need anything or if I can be of any help. You know you are one of best employees." She gave me a big smile and a wink.

"I know. Thanks," I said, giving back the fakest smile I could muster up.

I walked back to my desk and instantly broke down. This was all just too much for me. I wasn't built for any of this. Before I could calm myself down, my co-worker, Peter, came over to my desk. Peter was real cool. He was a little bit older than I was, maybe twenty-three or twenty-four, but he already owned his own house and was engaged to be married. He was also a youth minister at his church, but that didn't stop him from flirting with me every chance he got. He wasn't a bad looking dude and he damn sure could dress, but soon-to-be married men would never be an option of mine, so I always shut down his attempts. Other than the annoying flirting, Peter was cool to talk to and he gave great advice, so I decided to vent. I needed to get this shit off my chest before I exploded. I told him everything from Q being locked up to me needing $1,000 to bail him out.

"Wow, V, that sucks. I'm really sorry to hear that. So, what are you going to do? You can't just leave him in there."

"I don't know what I'm gonna do, but I do know I don't have $1,000 right now and I don't plan on having an extra $1,000 anytime soon. None of his family will help and I refuse to ask my mother for another dime. I really, really just don't know what I'm gonna do." Right then, his phone began to ring so he excused himself and walked back over to his desk. A few minutes later, the notification on my computer alerting me that I had an email chimed. It was from Peter, which I thought was weird because he could've easily just come back over to my desk if he wanted to finish our conversation. I opened the email and proceeded to read it.

Hey, You,

I just wanted to say again that I'm really sorry about what you're going through right now. You're a really nice, beautiful girl and you don't deserve to be going through any of this. I know you said that you need $1,000 to bail your boyfriend out; I might be able to help you out with that, but the question is, what are you willing to do in return? How bad do you want this boyfriend of yours out? Think about it and let me know... ;)

Pete

What was I willing to do?

Chapter 21

I must have read the email a thousand times before looking away from my computer. I looked across the office at Peter, expecting to see a big smile plastered on his face or him dying laughing at his own joke, but instead, he was staring at me with a devilish grin and lust in eyes. This nigga was dead serious. I looked back and forth from my computer screen to his stupid grin as I mentally weighed my options. *It's not like he's ugly or like he'd be dumb enough to tell anyone. One time couldn't hurt, right,* I thought to myself. But just as quickly as the thoughts occurred, they were gone. I had to check myself. Is this what my life had become? At this point, I wasn't even mad that Peter had basically offered me $1,000 for some pussy. Instead, I was mad at the fact that for a moment, I was considering it. But then I remembered that my momma didn't raise a whore, nor did she raise a weak ass bitch with no standards. I rolled my eyes at Peter with the meanest grill I could muster up and then turned back to my computer screen. I hit the respond button.

Peter,

First and foremost, you are very disrespectful for the email you just sent me. I'm not sure what kind of female you think I am, but let's make something clear. Never have I and never will I be desperate enough to have sex for money. And especially not with a man who claims he's soon-to-be married. Oh, and let's not forget that you also claim to be a man of God. HA! I wonder how your soon-to-be wife would feel about this email because you and I both already know how God feels about it. So, here's some advice for you. The next time you want to be a creep, you might want to reconsider leaving a trail in your well-monitored WORK email. And the next time you think you can come at me, please come correct! Good day!

Victoria

I clicked send and got back to work. Clearly, this nigga had me twisted and I was not about to entertain his foolery. I kept hearing the chime for my email alert going off as I was working; all the messages were from Peter. I opened the first one and started to read it.

Victoria,

Let me first start by saying my intentions were absolutely not to disrespect you in any way. You know how I feel about you...

I couldn't even finish reading it after that part. This nigga had a whole lot of nerve talking about how he "feels about me" when he had a whole fucking fiancé at home. From that point on, I just erased every one of his emails without even opening or reading them. If he kept it up, I was going to start forwarding them to our boss. I'm sure she would have a lot to say about him sexually harassing me right under her nose. Around lunchtime, he even tried to come over to my desk and apologize, but I quickly dismissed him. I wasn't even trying to hear it. The damage was already done.

"Victoria, please just let me explain," he begged.

"Boy, if you don't step away from my desk, I swear to God I'ma get fired today for steeling on you." I looked up from my computer right into his eyes so he could know I was dead serious.

"Steeling on me? What does that mean?" I rolled my eyes.

"Just get the fuck away from my desk, Peter. Thank you." He walked away with his head hung low. *Stupid ass.*

I kept myself busy the entire day and before I knew it, it was time to clock out, pick up Aaliyah, and head home to freshen up for our visit with Q. This would be the first time I ever visited someone in jail, so I had no idea what I could or couldn't wear. But what I did know was that Aaliyah and I would be fresh regardless. No one would ever catch us slipping, not even at a jail visit. I arrived at the jail at about 7:15 PM. After going through security and securing our stuff in a locker, I sat nervously on a hard bench, waiting to be called. I kept telling myself "no tears, V" but I could already feel them building up as I thought about how fucked up my life had turned in such a short period of time. The sad part was I couldn't even blame anyone but myself.

"Visit for Scott." That was us. I followed the manly looking woman corrections officer into a small room that had four booths, each containing two phones separated by glass. Through the glass, I could see a large area set up with tables, chairs, one TV, and lots of inmates walking around, socializing. I was a little disappointed by the glass separation. I just knew that I was going to be able to hug Q when I saw him. The fact that I wouldn't be able to had tears threatening to fall. I fought to hold them back as I looked down at my feet. I was so in my feelings that I didn't even notice Q walking over until Aaliyah started jumping up and down, pointing and smiling.

"Q! Q! Q, mommy! Q!" she cheered in her little voice.

I looked up at Q and tears began to fall. I had never seen my baby looking so rough and worn down since I had known him. He faintly smiled at Aaliyah and then played peek-a-boo, shielding his face with his hands. She loved when he did that. He picked up the phone and I followed suit.

"Hey, bae. You aight?" he asked just as I was about to ask him.

"I'm OK, I guess. Just worried sick about you. How are you holding up in here?"

"Shit, I'm aight. Just hungry as fuck and missing y'all like crazy, but I'll be aight. You do everything I asked you to do?"

"Yeah, I did. Yo' bail is $1,000 cash," I responded, looking away.

"Yeah, I know. I found out today when my lawyer came to see me. What was my moms saying when you hit her up?"

"Nothing really. Keep her posted. Were you expecting her to say much of anything?" If I knew better when it came to her, I was sure he did too.

"Nah, not really. I was just asking." I could hear the disappointment in his voice, so I changed the subject to avoid an awkward moment.

"Can you tell me what the hell all of this is about, please?"

"To be honest, not really. These folks are def monitoring these visits, waiting for a nigga to slip up on some info. But what I can tell you is that I need to bail me out ASAP so I can get some shit in order for the future. Tomorrow after work, I want you to pawn my PlayStation and all my games. It's down the street. Tell them I sent you. And then pawn whatever else you can find too. I wish I didn't have my jewels on me when I got bagged 'cause we would be straight right now, but fuck it. Let's just work with what we do have."

I rolled my eyes. Q was telling me absolutely nothing about the situation at hand except for what he needed me to do. I felt like I was running around doing these things and didn't even know the reason behind any of it. It was frustrating the shit out of me, but for now, I would try to be supportive and cooperate.

"OK. What is it that you need to get in order for the future? Maybe I can help with that too."

"Nah, don't even worry about none of that right now, shawty. I just need you to focus on getting me up outta here and then preparing yourself to ride this thing out with me until the wheels fall off." Red flag. I was starting to get the feeling that Q was hiding something major and very important about this situation.

"Until the wheels fall off? What does that mean?" I tilted my head to the side and gave him a confused look.

"That means that this ain't no shit that's just gonna go away overnight, Victoria." I could hear the annoyance in his voice, but I didn't care. I was going to get me some answers one way or another.

"OK. So, when will it go away? Can you just be real with me, damn?" I hated when people beat around the bush and sugarcoated shit. I wanted the truth, not some fucking fairytale lie. I could tell my attitude was starting to frustrate him.

"Aight, check it. If this shit goes to the left and my lawyer can't get me off, I'm looking at three years. Now what?" I wanted to respond, but I had no idea what to say, so I sat there silently, looking stuck on stupid.

"Yeah, exactly what I thought. You can't handle the truth, shawty. It's aight, though, 'cause as soon as I get out of here, I'ma take care of all of this, feel me? So just do whatever you gotta do to get me up outta here and I promise you I got us, lil mama." The phone shut off and the corrections officer walked in, yelling that the visit was over. Aaliyah and I placed our hands on the window parallel to Q's as he and I mouthed *I love you* to one another. When I picked Aaliyah up to leave, she started fighting me and crying, reaching for Q. I could tell seeing her like that was breaking his heart, so I put some pep in my step and got out of there before all three of us were crying.

On the ride home, and for the rest of the night, Q's last words to me kept ringing in my head. "Do whatever you gotta do to get me up outta here and I promise you I got us, lil mama." He said whatever, but I knew there was no way he meant *whatever whatever*. Or did he? I instantly began to think about the offer that Peter had made me earlier that day. I knew I had gone off and acted like a straight bitch to him after his little email, but I also knew the power of the pussy. So, regardless of how mean I had been to him, I knew if I threw my pussy at him, he would still catch it. Getting him to agree again would be the easy part, but the hard part was deciding if I could live with myself after. I grabbed a bottle of Cîroc out of the cabinet and decided I would drink until I could convince myself that I was brave enough to do this; for Q. He needed me.

Chapter 22

The next day, I woke up feeling determined and ready. I looked through my closet for the shortest, tightest, yet still work-appropriate skirt I could find. I matched it with a sheer sleeveless blouse, a fitted blazer, and six-inch black leather pumps. I put some pearls in my ear and slicked my hair up into a neat sock bun to tone it down a bit. But then I added a red lip to my usual eyeliner and mascara to tone it back up. Even with a slight hangover from last night's drinking, I was looking like a bad bitch. I was ready to go get this money and bring my man home.

I dropped Aaliyah off at school and pulled up to work fifteen minutes early. I knew my boss wouldn't be in yet because Peter opened on Wednesdays. I figured this would be my opportunity to get my flirt on and reel Peter back in. When I walked in the office, he was on a phone call at his desk. I strutted by, putting an extra switch in my hips and gave him a quick wink as I headed towards my desk. And just like I expected, his thirsty ass immediately ended his phone call and came running over to my desk like the little puppy that he was. Now, it was show time.

"Good morning, Pete," I purred. "I just wanted to apologize to you about yesterday. This stuff with my boyfriend really, really has my emotions all over the place. I didn't mean to snap at you like that. I hope you can forgive me." I looked down, pouting and playing the role. I was almost positive someone would be giving me an Oscar after this performance.

"Of course, I forgive you, love." He lifted my chin so that I was looking at him. "Don't even worry about it. I understand." He licked his lips, trying to be sexy. I wanted to burst out laughing, but I had to keep it cool in order for this to work in my favor.

"Well, to be honest, I was really shocked to find out that you were even interested in me like that." I looked away again as if I was shy.

"Girl, are you crazy? How the hell wouldn't I be interested in you like that? As fine as you are? Shit, every nigga that comes through that door wishes they had a chance with you and if they don't, they're either blind or gay."

"Awwww, that's so sweet of you, Pete," I said, rubbing his arm. He blushed.

"No problem. I'm just speaking the truth. I know I may have come off a little too strong yesterday, but that's just 'cause I figured…" At that moment, my boss came strolling in, so I whispered to Peter "email me" and turned to my desk to pretend like I had been doing work. Not even five minutes later, my email alert chimed. I opened the email from Peter.

Hey,

So, like I was saying. I've been feeling you and I didn't mean any disrespect yesterday. I really didn't. I just figured that I could help you out with your situation and you could make my dream come true all at the same time. Two birds, one stone, right? ☺

I hit respond.

Oh, okay. I hear what you saying. I'm flattered that you consider me a dream come true. That's really sweet. I also appreciate you being willing to help a sista out. What you're saying makes sense, but what about your girl? Won't she be mad if she finds out?

I knew I shouldn't have even brought his girl up, but I just had to. The guilt inside me wouldn't let me not remind this nigga yet again that he was engaged to be married. Now all I could do was pray I didn't fuck up my chances by being so thoughtful. I opened his response.

She's cool with it, but she doesn't have to join if you don't want her to. She doesn't mind sitting on the sidelines and watching while we do our thing. So how about we stop wasting time. How's tonight around 8 sound? We can chill at my place. Wear something sexy.

Wait, what? I stared at the computer screen for a few minutes, trying to make sure I read his response correctly. Peter was officially on some other shit and I wanted no parts of any of it. I couldn't believe this nigga went from trying to buy pussy from me to trying to have a threesome with his fiancé AND buy pussy all at the same damn time. Or maybe it was just the threesome he was trying to pay for, but either way, I was all set. But for now, I decided to try my hardest to hide my disgust in my response, just in case.

I'm not sure if I'll be able to find a sitter on such short notice. It is a weekday, but I'll see what I can do and keep you posted. Let me get back to work, though. I have like a million unread emails to sort through. Lata handsome! ☺

I looked over to see if he had fallen for my excuse and from the big smile on his face, he did. *Sucker.* The rest of my shift I avoided Peter as best as I could. I even went as far as to ask my boss if I could leave an hour early. I was starting to feel smothered I needed to get away and clear my head before I headed to my afternoon classes. Plus, I could use the extra time to go to the pawnshop like Q had told me to the night before.

****

I drove over to Q's apartment and rang the bell. I knew even though he was locked up, all his boys would still be there chilling because that's all their asses did all damn day. After waiting for about five minutes, his homeboy Tony finally opened the door.

"Hey, V! What you doing here, ma? Wassup with Q? You ain't heard from him yet?" He looked me up and down, not even trying to hide the lust all over his face. I rolled my eyes. I hated this nigga's New York accent almost as much as I hated him. I couldn't understand for the life of me why Q trusted him. He had grimy written all over his forehead in big, bold letters. But since he was Q's connect, I tolerated him.

"Hey. Yeah, I heard from Q. He's straight. His bail is a stack, though," I responded dryly.

"Damn, for real? He ain't say what the charges were when you spoke to him, did he?" I wasn't feeling his vibes at all. I wanted to rash on his fraud ass for fake caring, but I refrained.

"Nah, he ain't get into all that. But he did give me some instructions, which is why I'm here. Now, can you let me in, please?" The nerve of this nigga, having me standing outside on the porch like this wasn't my man's crib.

"Oh, oh. My fault, my fault. Come in, ma." I could feel him fucking me with his eyes as I pushed past him into the smoke-filled apartment. There were two dudes sitting on the couch that I recognized and one that I didn't. I felt a little nervous being there by myself, but I kept my game face on.

"So, what can I do for you, ma? You said something about some instructions or some shit like that." I wanted to tell his ugly ass to mind his fucking business, but I didn't.

"Yeah, last night, Q told me to come over here and get his PlayStation and games to take to the pawnshop. We need the money to put towards his bail since ain't nobody else stepping up to the plate." I was throwing major shade towards everybody in the room. They all claimed to be his boys, but not one of them had asked if they could help in any way. Fake ass niggas. Without saying anything else, I started gathering up Q's games that were tossed around the living room area. The sooner I got the fuck up out of there, the better.

"Oh, I see. Well, unfortunately, I can't even let you do that, ma. Actually, we were just about to play a few games of NBA Live after we rotated this blunt. That PlayStation is the trap's, not Q's." I paused in my steps. I turned to look at him to see if he was joking, but his facial expression told me that he was dead serious.

"The trap's PlayStation? So, that means the owner of the trap paid for it, right? And whose trap is this exactly?"

"Mine," he responded with a big, stupid grin. All the other dudes in the room began to laugh, but I didn't find shit funny.

"Yours? Oh, really? Since when? 'Cause I've seen the lease and I don't see yo' name nowhere on that shit!" I knew there was a reason I couldn't stand this nigga from the time I laid eyes on him.

"Well, to be honest, ma, without me, there would be no trap, you feel me?"

"No, I don't feel you. But what I do feel is that without Q, there would be no fucking PlayStation, so like I said, I'm taking it and I'm taking the games like I was instructed." I was over all this back and forth shit.

"No, you not," he responded, walking up on me. I looked at him like he was crazy. I couldn't believe this nigga had the nerve to be trying to intimidate me. Unfortunately, for him, he caught me on the wrong day. My adrenaline was pumping and I was ready for whatever. I had one goal and that was to bring my man home and I damn sure wasn't about to let Tony stand in the way of that. I didn't even respond. Instead, I continued picking up all the equipment and games that were in plain sight and headed for the door. Before I opened the door to leave, I looked back at Tony. If looks could kill, I would definitely be six feet under.

"Who's gonna stop me?" I asked, grilling him right back, and then I left. I threw all the stuff in the back of my car and pulled off quickly in case this nigga wanted to try some dumb shit. I still couldn't even believe he had went as hard as he did for a PlayStation. *Wait until I tell Q this shit!*

Chapter 23

Now that I had Q's stuff, it was time to rummage around my own apartment and see what else I could find to bring with me to the pawnshop. After searching all over, all I could come up with was a few pieces of gold jewelry I never wore, two DVD players, and the 14-inch flat screen TV from Aaliyah's room. I felt guilty about pawning her TV, but I reminded myself that her ass barely watched it to help with that. If she wasn't in my bed watching TV, she was on the living room floor, taking over that TV instead. Long story short, she would be alright.

There were a few pawnshops in the area, but since hadn't told me which one in particular I should go to, I just stopped at the first one that I saw. I felt so embarrassed struggling to lug all my belongings from the car to the hole in the wall shop. I did what I had to do though because, at this point, time was ticking.

"Excuse me," I said to the ghetto girl behind the window. She was talking extra loud on her cell phone about somebody's baby daddy trying to holla at her. I found that hard to believe, though. Everything about her screamed hood rat. From her long acrylic nails to her blue weave and one front gold tooth.

"EXCUSE ME!" I said again a little louder this time. *I know this bitch sees and hears me,* I thought. She looked over at me and sucked her teeth and then rolled her eyes extra hard. *No this bitch didn't!*

"Girl, let me call you back. I gotta customer." She hung up her phone and strutted over to the window with an attitude all over her face.

"Yeah?" I chuckled at her rudeness to keep from going off on her.

"Hey, how are you today? I would like to pawn a few items for some cash, please." I was going to kill her ugly ass with kindness today.

"Lemme see what you got." I handed her over my items and watched her head to the back of the store. I was praying like hell she wasn't the one pricing my stuff because she didn't even look or sound like she could do math, let alone estimate the monetary value of something. To my relief, an older black man came from another room in the shop and started to sort through my items while little Miss Ghetto-tude came back over to the window.

"You gon' have to give us a minute. You can go sit over there." She pointed to a rundown couch in the corner that I wouldn't sit on even if someone paid me to.

"Nah, that's okay. I'll wait in my car. I'll come back in about twenty minutes."

"Whatever." I ignored her ignorant ass and headed for the door. As soon as I walked away, she was right back on her cell phone, running her mouth.

"Yeah, girl, my bad. Some bougie ass bitch just walked up in here tryna be all cute and shit." I smiled. If I were her bum ass, I would hate on me too.

****

Twenty minutes later, I walked back into the shop and guess who was still on their cell phone, running their mouth without a care in the world. And this time, she had the nerve to have a line of people waiting. I shook my head and tapped the elderly lady in front of me, asking how long she had been standing there waiting. She said about five to ten minutes. Ridiculous. Just then, the older man who I had seen earlier came out from the back and Miss

Ghetto-tude hung up her phone quickly, acting like she had been working the whole time. The shit was comedy. Of course, when I got up to the window, she still had her funky ass attitude, but just like before, I was kind and polite. Ugly bitches hated pretty and kind girls.

"We don't need yo' DVD players so you can have those back and we giving you $500 cash for the rest."

"Five hundred dollars? That's it? For a TV, a damn near brand new PlayStation and all my jewelry? That stuff has to come up to at least $800. You bugging!" I was beyond tight.

"Look, you want the money or not? I got other customers waiting, so I ain't about to argue with you. It's your choice!" I wanted to remind this rude broad that she damn sure wasn't thinking about those other customers when she was running her mouth on her cell phone, but I calmed myself down quickly. I had to remember that there was a purpose to all this; Q needed this money.

"I'll take it."

"Ummhmmm." She rolled her eyes and handed me the cash. I walked away, feeling defeated yet again. As soon as I got to my car, I burst into tears. I really thought I would come close to the amount I needed to bail Q out, but instead, I was a whole $500 short. I was supposed to be heading to class, but opted out and headed home instead. I was a wreck. There was no way I would be able to focus in school. I walked into my apartment and headed directly for my couch. I laid there for what seemed like hours crying and asking God why me.

I had been trying so hard the past few days to keep it together, but now I felt like I was out of options. Payday was in two days, but rent was due in less than a week. There was no way I could afford to pay my rent, my childcare, and bail Q out all with one check. Plus, we needed some groceries in the house. Asking my mother for money was absolutely not an option and neither was the freaky shit Peter was trying to talk me into. There had to be another way.

The sound of my phone ringing snapped me out of my thoughts. It was Q. That made me smile a little through my tears. Words couldn't explain how bad I was missing him. As soon as the call connected, I tried my hardest to disguise the fact that I had just been crying.

"Hi, baby! What took you so long to call me? I've been waiting to hear from you all day. Is everything okay?"

"Sorry, babe. They weren't tryna let us use the phones until right now. I'm aight, though, but I see you still over there crying. Didn't I tell you there ain't no time for that right now? We gon' be aight, V, for real. I need you to trust me, shawty." I chuckled at how this man knew me like the back of his hand. I couldn't hide anything from him if I wanted to.

"I'm sorry, babe. It's just so hard not having you here. But you're right. No more crying, I swear." I knew I was lying, but oh well.

"Aight. And I just thought of something. Shouldn't you be in class right now?" Busted.

"Yeah, I should be, but I just couldn't today. My emotions are all over the place right now."

"No excuses, shawty. I can't have you missing school or work. I need you to be strong and keep yo' head up. Have some faith in yo' man, aight? Now, did you at least go to the pawnshop today since you at home chilling and shit." I knew he was trying to make me laugh, so I did.

"Yes, I just came back from there a little while ago actually. They only gave me $500, though."

"Aight, cool. That's a start. When we hang up, hit up Tony and see if he can throw something towards that. Tell him I said I got him once I touch down. He knows I'm good for it."

"Fuck Tony! Real talk!" Just the mention of his name had my blood boiling.

"Damn, I know you don't be feeling him like that, but what's all that about?" It killed me how clueless Q was about what type of nigga Tony real is.

"What it's about is the fact that your so-called homeboy wasn't even tryna let me take anything from your spot to help get you out. He was talking all types of crazy, saying it was his crib and some more shit. AND he had the nerve to be doing it in front of other people. Straight disrespectful. But that's your boy, though," I said sarcastically.

"Man, chill out. He was probably just fucking with you. But I know how you be getting all serious and shit over nothing just 'cause you don't like him." *So, now it's my fault his nigga ain't shit,* I thought to myself.

"No, he wasn't playing, Quincy. He was dead serious. But whatever. I'll let you see who that nigga really is for yourself, but in the meantime, I am not asking him for shit. Point. Blank. Period." Q could be mad if he wanted to, but I wasn't doing it.

"Aight, aight, relax. Just hit up my moms again and see what she can do. And baby, I know you really, really don't want to, but you might have to hit up your moms too. I gotta get outta here. The sooner I do, the better things will be. Tell her I'll even pay her back within a month. I just need her to help me out this one time." I could hear the desperation in his voice and it hurt my heart. I told him okay, even though I already knew his mother wasn't coming up off any dough and I damn sure wasn't asking my mother. He was still talking, but I was so zoned out in my thoughts that I completely missed everything else he had just said.

"Victoria, you hear me?"

"Huh? Yeah, I hear you, babe."

"Aight. Well, this phone is about to hang up. I love you. Kiss Aaliyah for me when you pick her up."

"I love you too and I will."

The call ended and I sat there, staring into space. My phone vibrated, letting me know that it was time to go get Aaliyah. I was surprised when I picked up my phone to see that it wasn't my alarm; it was a text message from Jason. We had texted back and forth a few times since I had bumped into him, but every time he mentioned us hanging out, I ended the conversation. Out of curiosity, I opened up the text.

Still waiting for my chance… I'll wait forever if I have to…

I read it twice and then pressed delete. I then went into my contacts and deleted him out of my contacts altogether. I had enough shit on my plate right now; I didn't need the distraction.

I grabbed my purse to head out to go get Aaliyah. Before I pulled off, I texted Q's mom and let her know that I had half the money and was wondering if she could put anything towards what I already had. She responded that she would see what she could do and I already knew what that meant. I didn't even bother to respond back because if I did, I might just tell her about herself. Instead, I just accepted the fact that asking for help from people was pointless in this particular situation. This shit right here was all on Q and me. Bonnie and Clyde 2008 shit.

Chapter 24

"OH SHIT!" I jumped up and grabbed my cell phone off the nightstand. It was 10:03 AM and I was scheduled to be at work at 8 AM today. I had completely overslept, which I never ever did. I guess the stress and the sleepless nights were starting to take a toll on my mind and my body. I had already missed half of my shift, so getting myself and Aaliyah ready just drive through loads of Atlanta traffic would be pointless. By the time I got to work, my shift would be damn near over since I was off at 12 PM. With that being said, I snuggled up with a still sleeping Aaliyah and dozed back into dreamland. Twenty minutes later, she was jumping up and down on the bed, demanding I make her breakfast. So much for sleeping in.

I headed into the kitchen to make me and my baby some waffles and scrambled eggs with cheese, her favorite. I thought about calling my boss to apologize for not calling or showing up, but I decided against it. I would deal with her tomorrow as soon as I clocked in; that way, I could explain myself face to face. I also decided that I wasn't going to my classes again today. All I wanted to do all day was lay in bed with my princess while watching cartoons. I needed a mental health day and time to figure out what my next moves were going to be.

The alert on my cell phone went off, notifying me that I had received a text message. It was from my mother.

Good morning baby girl. Just texting you to see if everything is OK. I haven't heard from you in a few days...

Everything definitely wasn't okay. In fact, it was the total fucking opposite, but there was no way I could tell her that. This time I was determined to clean up my own mess like the grown woman I claimed to be.

Sorry mommy. I've just been really, really busy with work and school. Everything is okay tho' ☺

I thought that sounded convincing enough.

Are you sure, Victoria?

I guess not.

Yes, mommy. I'm sure. Gotta get back to work tho'. I'll call you later. Love you.

Okay, make sure you call please. Love you too.

I knew my mother was no dummy. She knew something was wrong and I knew that when it was all said and done, she would make it her business to find out just like any other time. But for now, I planned to keep her in the dark for as long as possible.

✱✱

Around noon, Aaliyah and I were laying in bed, watching *Dora the Explorer,* when my phone started ringing. It was Q. I wondered why he was calling so early, but then I remembered that he knew my schedule like the back of his hand, which meant he knew I had an hour of free time from 12 to 1 today before my classes started. *Awwww.* I couldn't help but cheese while listening to the automated recording.

"Hey, babyyyyyy. I'm so happy you called. I've been missing you like crazy," I purred into the phone as soon as the call was connected.

"Hey, shawthee. Watthup wit' it?" was his response; no enthusiasm whatsoever.

"Well damn. I guess I'm the only one doing the missing around here, huh?" I rolled my eyes like he could see me.

"Nah, it ain't even like that I promith you." That's when I noticed the difference in the pronunciation of his words. It almost sounded like his mouth was full or something.

"Quincy, are you eating in my ear? You know how much I hate that shit."

"Nah, I ain't eating. To be honest, I haven't really eaten since I've been in here."

"Okay. So, if you not eating, why does it sound like your mouth is full?"

"'Cause it is. Don't start tripping, V, but last night, I got jumped."

The room started to spin as I struggled to let out the breath that I had just taken in. It was a good thing I was already in bed because I was sure I would be on the floor by now if I wasn't.

"You got what? What are you talking about, Quincy? Jumped for what? Jumped by who?" Q wasn't the type of nigga who had beef out in these streets. He was a real down to earth dude who mostly stayed to himself. And he damn sure didn't start drama, so him getting jumped made no sense to me.

"Look, I don't know who jumpth me and I don't know why they jumpth me. And even if I did, I wouldn't say it over this phone, so chill with all the questions, aight? What I do know is that I gotta get the fuck outta here ASAP. I can't stay here through the weekend, V. Real shit."

I tried my hardest to disguise the whimpers along with the tears that I was fighting back. Shit was getting realer by the day.

And yet and still, we were still stuck with no clear way out. We needed a miracle to get us out of this fucked up situation.

"Yo', they abouth to lock us in, but I just called to let you know what was up. I got visits again later today. See if Miss Rayna will keep Aaliyah for an extra hour today while you stop by and see me real quick. I don't want baby girl to see me looking like this." I couldn't hold it in anymore. I broke down right at that moment. This shit was beyond crazy.

"VICTORIA!" Q snapped at me.

"Cuth that shit out yo', for real. I'll see you tonight, aight? And if you can't come, I'll call your phone around 9. Try to geth up here, though. I need to kick it witchu. I love you." The call disconnected before I could respond.

"Mommy don't cry. Why you cry?" Aaliyah said while rubbing the tears on my face with her little hands. I smiled at her through my tears and wrapped her in my arms. No matter what I was currently going through, one thing never changed, and that was how perfect my baby was. If it weren't for anyone else, I had to pull it together for her sake.

"Mommy's okay, baby. How about we eat some lunch and take a nap? Mommy is still sleepy and very hungry. You want rice?"

"YAAAYYYY, RICE!" she yelled, jumping up and down on my bed. I scooped her up and headed to the kitchen to chef us up some lunch before naptime.

****

While Aaliyah lay sprawled out across my bed, belly nice and full, I sat up, thinking of my next move. Based on the conversation I had with Q earlier in the day, it seemed like I only had until tomorrow to come up with five hundred more dollars. If something else bad happened to him while he was in there, I wouldn't be able to forgive myself. Shit, I was already struggling to accept the fact that he had been jumped the night before.

An hour later, Aaliyah started stirring in her sleep, which let me know she was about to wake up. Yet, I had no plan other than to come clean to my mother about what was going on and hope she let me borrow the money. With my luck, she would be on her way down here to bring Aaliyah and me back to Boston, leaving Q stuck to fend for himself. Because I knew that was a highly possible reaction, I decided to hold off on calling and asking her until after my visit with Q. Hopefully, he had a better plan because my plan might just be the reason that he didn't get out this weekend.

Aaliyah's teacher, Miss Rayna, had agreed to watch her for an hour off the record after I lied and told her I was having a family emergency and needed to run to the hospital to check on things. I dropped Aaliyah off and headed to the jail to see Q before I missed visiting hours for the day.

When Q walked in, I almost fell off my hard metal seat. *No wonder he didn't want me to bring Yaya,* I thought to myself. He had a busted lip, a bandage over his left eye and from what I could see, he was walking with a slight limp. I wanted so badly to reach out and embrace him and hold him close, but the glass between us made that impossible. He picked up the phone.

"It ain't even as bad as it looks, shawty, don't trip." I just nodded my head, scared that if I tried to speak the tears would start flowing.

"There's only about fifteen minutes left for visits, so let me get straight to business. I think I know a way you can get the rest of the money to get me out by tomorrow." My ears instantly perked up hearing this.

"When is the rent due?" he asked.

"Monday."

"Yeah, that's what I thought. Cool. You remember that gas station joke we always make around the first?" I tilted my head to the side with a confused look plastered on my face.

"Think about it." He was giving me a look that said he was trying to say more than he was verbally saying.

"Gas station joke. Gas station joke." I was lost. I had no idea what the hell Q could possibly be talking about. And I damn sure couldn't even start to imagine how some joke was going to help me get him out by tomorrow. After awhile, he started to get annoyed with the fact that I wasn't catching on to what he was trying to say.

"Victoria, you acting real slow today, shawty, and its pissing me off. Straight up. So, what I want you to do after you leave this visit is go home, take a hot shower, clear your mind and get that shit right 'cause right now ain't the time for you to be acting lost. I'm depending on you to figure this shit out, shawty. And when you do, you'll know what you need to do. I love you."

"I love you too," I responded with my head down as we were both escorted out of the visitation booths.

****

I drove in silence to pick up Aaliyah. I was still racking my brain trying to figure out Q's little gas station riddle. When I got there, I thanked Miss Rayna and headed right back home, still driving in silence and thinking. I looked at my dashboard and noticed that my gas light was on. There was a gas station a few blocks from Aaliyah's daycare that I usually went to, so I stopped there. Just that quickly, Aaliyah had dozed off, so I left her in the car while I ran inside to pay for my gas.

"Well, good evening, pretty lady. How are you this evening?" I smiled. It never failed. The Indian guy who worked the register at this station was forever flirting with me. Even on my worst days.

"Hey, love. Let me get ten on three, please."

"Anything for you, pretty lady," he said in his strong Indian accent while punching in the amount on his computer. He seductively grabbed the ten-dollar bill from my hand and stuck it in the register without even looking at it. He never took his eyes off me. This happened every time I went there, even if Q was with me. I shook my head and chuckled as I headed back to my car to pump my gas.

"OH SHIT!"

I stopped dead in my tracks. Now I knew exactly what Q wanted me to do.

Chapter 25

Last night I barely got any sleep. The realization of what Q wanted me to do started to sink in and had me feeling sick to my stomach with fear. I knew desperate times called for desperate measures, but damn, he could've at least came up with an idea that wouldn't potentially send my ass to jail right with him. I wasn't scary or anything like that. Before I moved to Atlanta, I had even boosted a few outfits a few times with Trina. But this right here could get me in some serious trouble and I knew it.

I sat on the edge of my bed, trying to mentally and physically push myself to head out the door before I was late for work. I was praying that my boss didn't trip too much about my no call, no show yesterday. Since I had been working there, I had never been late nor had I ever called out, even when I was sick. If my history as a great employee didn't help me out, my last resort was to turn on the water works right there at her desk. My boss was a nice woman and she really liked me. I was sure she would hate to see me crying like my world was about to end.

I pulled up to Aaliyah's at-home daycare and was greeted by her teacher at the door. I walked Aaliyah inside, put away her diaper bag and gave her a big hug and kiss.

"Mommy's gonna see you later, OK, big girl?"

"Yes, mama. We see Q?" She had been asking me this same question every single day since we visited Q and every single time it brought tears to my eyes. The love Aaliyah had for Q in such a short amount of time might have even been greater than the love I had for him. Instead of responding, I just hugged her tightly and gave a great big kiss on her forehead. She pulled on my neck so that I would bend down more to her height. When I did, she kissed me back on my forehead. We both laughed.

As I was heading out the door, Aaliyah's teacher grabbed me by the shoulder to stop me.

"Can I have a word with you?" she asked politely. I instantly felt nervous but shook my head yes.

"Is everything OK with Aaliyah?" I was praying it was because I damn sure couldn't take any more bad news, especially not bad news about my baby.

"Yes, ma'am. Aaliyah is fine."

"I just wanted to bring it to your attention that you're more than a week behind on your childcare. That normally isn't like you, so I figured I would just give you a heads-up face to face instead of sending a slip home like I do with the other parents." There was embarrassment written all over my face. She was right. That wasn't like me. Until now, I hadn't even realized that I was behind. I quickly apologized and told her I would have a payment for her when I returned to pick Aaliyah up. This was just one more unexpected cost that I couldn't afford.

✳✳

After I had dropped Aaliyah off, I pulled into the parking lot of my job and I immediately got this queasy feeling in my stomach like something wasn't right. *Maybe that's just my stomach growling since I skipped breakfast and dinner last night.* I shook the feeling off, parked my car and went inside. Once inside, I headed straight to my boss' office to explain myself. I figured it would be better if I went to her rather than her coming to speak to me. Her door was slightly closed, so I knocked.

"Hey, Maria, do you have a quick minute?" She looked up from the paperwork on her desk and gave me this weird expression. I instantly got the queasy feeling in my stomach again.

"Oh, sure, Victoria. I was just about to call your desk to see if you had made it in yet. I wasn't sure if you were coming in today considering the fact that you never showed up for your shift yesterday or called to say you weren't coming as far as I know. I have to be honest, I was very worried about you, but seeing that you look physically okay, I am now more disappointed than anything. I would've never expected a no call, no show from you. You have been a great employee here up until recently. I know you told me earlier this week that you've been having some family issues, but unfortunately, that is no excuse." I nodded my head in agreement.

"You are absolutely right, Maria, and I want to apologize for yesterday without making any excuses. Nevertheless, I can reassure you that what occurred yesterday will never happen again. I can give you my word on that." She gave me a slight smile.

"I believe you, Victoria, I do, but unfortunately, we had a surprise visit from the owner of the company yesterday. Not only did he witness you not showing up and not calling to say that you wouldn't be in, he also performed a mini-audit for this week and all of your numbers were off." She looked away.

"My numbers were off? My numbers are NEVER off!" See, now this bitch was playing games. My numbers had always been on point from the time I finished my original training. How convenient it was that she was claiming that they were all of a sudden off.

"Yes, Victoria, your numbers were never off, until now. So, due to you not showing up yesterday without any notification, as well as your numbers being off, the owner has notified me that I have to let you go. I have your check right here from the past two weeks and will mail your check for the hours that you worked this week to your home address. I'm sorry, but there is nothing I can do." She seemed genuinely sad that she had to do this to me.

"So you mean to tell me that you have no say in this situation at all?" Although she seemed genuine, I still found that kind of hard to believe. The owner of the company had never even met me, yet he got to fire me based on one visit. To me, that sounded a little suspect and unfair, to say the least.

"No, unfortunately, I don't. The decision has already been made."

All I could do was stare at her in disbelief. I had never been fired before and I never thought that I would be. I always gave my work 100% of my effort just like I did with my schoolwork. Not to mention right now was the worst time for this to be happening. I felt like I was going to pass out as what she had just said kept replaying in my head.

"You don't look too good, Victoria. Here, why don't you take your check and head home. I will still pay you as if you worked your entire shift." She handed me the envelope with my check in it. I silently took it from her hand, grabbed my purse off the chair I was sitting in and stood up to leave without saying another word. As I walked out of her office, I could hear her speaking to me, but I never looked back. Peter tried to stop me in my tracks, but I pushed right past him. I walked right out of the building without saying a word to anyone.

****

Before I could even make it to my car in the parking lot, my phone was vibrating. I looked at the caller ID and noticed it was the main number for my job. The first thing that crossed my mind was that Maria had already regretted firing me and was going to try and find a way to work around it. I quickly answered before I missed the call.

"Hello?"

"Hey, are you okay? I just heard about what happened." It was Peter. *I should've known it was his nosey ass!*

"Wow, word sure does spread fast. I literally just walked out of the door."

"Actually, I heard about it this morning before you even came in. I was gonna try and warn you, but you went straight to Maria's office when you came in so I didn't have a chance to say anything." I rolled my eyes on the other end of the phone. I didn't see why he was even calling me with his fake concern. I tried to end the conversation before he started asking questions.

"Yeah, I appreciate that, but I'm cool. Thanks for checking."

"You don't have to front for me, Victoria. I know you're not OK. For Christ sake, you just got fired, sweetheart. It's okay to be upset." I chuckled. This nigga thought he was so slick.

"Peter, what is your real purpose for being on my phone right now? And please don't say it's to see if I'm okay 'cause you and I both know that's not the case, so stop wasting my time and just say what you want." Real recognized real and I knew damn well that Peter's concern for me was as fake as my acrylic nails.

"Fine. I was just calling to see if being fired made you come to your senses about getting this $1,000. You're not a little girl anymore, Victoria. It's time to put on your big girl panties and live a little. Or should I say, take them off." He was such a creep it was disgusting. I hung up the phone before he could say anything else. Being fired may have been a blessing in disguise because there was no way I was going to be able to comfortably work with Peter with his behavior the past few days.

As soon as I finally got into my car, I ripped open the envelope, holding my check. I already knew how much it was supposed to be, but a small part of me was hoping for a miracle where the amount ended up being more than I expected. Nope. Only $750 like every two weeks. Six hundred dollars of that was for my rent. One hundred dollars was for Aaliyah's childcare. That left me with $50, which I would probably spend on gas and groceries. Great.

I stared at the check in my hand, realizing just how much my back was against the wall at this point. No money, no job, no man, no solution. Well, I had a solution if I listened to Q, but that shit came with lots of risks that I wasn't sure if I was willing to take. I looked over at the picture on my dashboard of me, Q, and Aaliyah. We looked so happy. I wanted that moment back. I needed it back. This was my family. At that moment, I decided I was done taking the good girl route. That shit wasn't getting me anywhere. If I wanted to get Q home, it was time to tune into my inner savage.

Chapter 26

My first stop was the joke shop on Memorial Road, not too far from my apartment complex. Now that I was really going to go through with this shit, I was going to need supplies. When I entered the store, I noticed that I was the only customer. I wasn't too surprised; it was only a little after 9 AM. Who the fuck is telling jokes that early? I was grateful that I was the only customer, though. The fewer people that saw me make my purchase, the better, just in case. I walked around the store until I found what I was looking for. I grabbed it and headed straight to the register without even looking at the price tag. Time was ticking and I needed to get this shit over and done with before I lost my nerve and changed my mind.

"Hi, how are you today, ma'am?" said the quirky little black boy at the register. He looked nervous as he fixed his broken glasses on his nose. *Damn, what, he'd never seen a pretty girl before or something,* I thought to myself.

"I'm good," I responded. I was in no mood to chit-chat and plus, his breath was humming, so the less talking we did, the better. I hoped that keeping my answers short would give him a hint that today wasn't the day so he should just do his damn job. Nope, didn't work.

"Beautiful day today, huh? The weather is so perfect I almost wish that I didn't have to work until five." He fixed his glasses again.

"Yeah, it's a nice day. But how much do I owe you for this? I'm kind of in a rush." Since he didn't catch my hint, I decided to be straightforward with his ass.

"Oh, okay. Sorry about that. Will this be all?" I sucked my teeth. I wanted to scream, "Obviously, this is all. Do you see me with anything else?" But instead, I just said yes and pulled out my wallet.

"That will be $12.99, please." I handed him a twenty-dollar bill and waited impatiently for my change.

"Here you go. Your change is $7.01. Now don't you go getting into any trouble with this. Remember, it's fake, even if it looks real." He gave me a stupid looking wink and then fixed his glasses again. I knew he was trying to make a joke, but his timing couldn't have been any worse. I don't know if it was my guilty conscience about what I was planning to do or the anger I felt about just being fired, but I instantly snapped.

"LOOK, LITTLE BOY, YOUR JOB IS TO ANSWER MY QUESTIONS AND RING UP MY SHIT, NOT WORRY ABOUT WHAT THE FUCK I'M GONNA DO WITH MY SHIT AFTER I PURCHASE IT, OKAY? NOW HAND ME MY DAMN BAG SO I CAN GO! I TOLD YOUR NOSEY ASS I WAS IN A RUSH, DIDN'T I? YET HERE YOU ARE, STILL TALKING MY DAMN EAR OFF! LEARN TO SHUT UP SOMETIMES WITH YOUR FUNKY ASS BREATH."

I snatched the bag out of his hand. He looked like he wanted to cry, but I didn't give a fuck. I stormed out of the door without even looking back and got in my car. My mother would be so ashamed if she ever saw me act like that in public. She definitely didn't raise me to behave so rudely and speak like that to someone who honestly did nothing to me but be friendly. But after all I had gone through and the way I was feeling right now, it was fuck the world because the world was most definitely fucking me. No lubricant.

I sat in my car, head on my steering wheel. My life felt like it was spiraling out of control. Just as I was about to start my car, my phone started to ring. It was the ring tone for an unknown call, so I figured it was Q. I pressed one to accept the call without giving the automatic lady a chance to say her whole script that I had heard a thousand times.

"Hey, baby, everything okay?" I asked once the call was connected.

"Damn, let me find out you moved to the A just to entertain jail birds."

"Excuse me? Who's this?" I didn't recognize the voice, but I knew it damn sure wasn't Q.

"Now you don't know my voice? Really, Victoria?" the unknown caller responded.

"Look, either say who the fuck you are or get the fuck off my phone! I'm in no mood for the games today, aight?" Whoever this person was must not have known who the fuck they were dealing with. I was never for the games and today damn sure wasn't the day to start.

"Chill out, gangsta. Where's my daughter at? That's the only reason I'm even calling your wack ass phone." It was Rich. I should have known.

"Wow. So, it takes for them to lock your black ass up for you to start caring about your daughter? We been gone five months and you ain't called once to check on her, but now all of a sudden, you calling. What you need, some canteen money or something?" I knew there was no way in hell that Rich went out of his way to call me from jail just to speak to Aaliyah. The nigga didn't even call on her birthday, yet here he was calling now.

"No. I just want to speak to my daughter like I said before. I know I haven't called, but that's 'cause I've been in here and wasn't nobody tryna deal with your drama. But I miss her, so I finally decided to just suck it up and call today. But from the way you answered the phone, I see I should've been called to check on my daughter's wellbeing. You fucking with jailbirds now, V?" I sucked my teeth. This nigga had some nerve.

"I'm sorry, ain't you in jail right now yourself? How the fuck are you calling anyone else a jailbird, dummy? I see you haven't gotten any smarter since we've been gone. And for your information, my man is no jailbird. He will be out today and has only been in a few days for some dumb shit. Small thing to some giants. What you locked up for? Some dumb shit, I'm guessing." I was halfway telling the truth and trying to change the subject, but I didn't care. I wasn't about to let Rich talk shit like he had one up on me or Q. He was a lame and he needed to know that.

"Don't worry about why I'm in here; it ain't your business. But as far as that nigga goes, yeah, yeah, yeah, that's what they all say. I don't care either way; I just wanna talk to my daughter. Don't nobody care about you or that lame ass nigga you over there taking care of."

"Whoa, whoa, whoa! Taking care of?" He said that last part too matter-of-factly for me to let it slide. He chuckled.

"You heard me. I bumped into Tee and she told me all about how you be down there taking care of that nigga. I guess everybody can't upgrade, right?" He started laughing at his own joke, which pissed me off even more than I already was.

"Nigga, fuck you. Don't worry about what the fuck I'm down here doing! How about you worry about why the next man is down here taking care of and playing daddy to your daughter. She probably doesn't even know who the fuck you are at this point. Matter fact, I don't know who the fuck you are either. Bye!" I hung my phone up.

I was pissed. I couldn't believe this nigga had just tried to talk shit when he hadn't done shit for his daughter in over a year. And then there was Tee. I was hurt that she would be going around spreading my business, especially to Rich, of all people. She knew I hated his ass. After all the shit I knew about her, I never ran her business. So, for her to run my business to an enemy of mine showed me that maybe our friendship wasn't where I thought it was after all. It was all good though because what I was about to do was going to get my man out and we were going to be straight. I was ready to ride this shit out until the wheels fell off. I went to start up my car again and my phone started ringing. I didn't even bother to listen for the ringtone.

"Who the fuck is it now?!" Now I was getting annoyed, for real. I looked at the name of the caller. It was Toya, just the person I wanted to speak to. I answered with an attitude purposely.

"Yo'."

"Uh-uh, bitch, do not be answering your phone like that for me! Especially when I haven't heard from your ass in days! You haven't even called to check on your godchild. You ain't shit!" She was so damn dramatic; I couldn't stand it.

"I've been busy. I heard you been busy too," I said sarcastically, referring to her running her mouth to Rich.

"Yeah, I bet you been busy. Busy sucking dick!" She and another person fell out laughing. My ears instantly perked up because the other voice sounded familiar.

"Who you with?" I was praying it wasn't who I thought it was.

"Trina. We in Target buying baby stuff." I shook my head. Toya was at an all-time low for this one.

"Really, Toya?" I said in an annoyed tone.

"What?" She knew exactly what, but was trying to act stupid like what she was doing wasn't wrong.

"So, you just fuck people's men and then have them baby shop with you, not knowing the baby might actually be their stepchild? That's cute." What Toya was doing right now was some real grimy shit. I couldn't respect it at all.

"What are you talking about, V? I already told you that wasn't even the case."

"Yeah, that's what your mouth say, but let's see what happens once that baby actually gets here. And honestly, whether it is Michael baby or not, you still fucked him, which is enough of a reason for you to not be chilling with Trina. That's trifling as hell and you know it, Toya." I was pissed to the point that you would've thought she fucked my man. I was big on principle and right now, Toya was straight up wrong. Just like she was wrong for running my business to Rich.

"You need to relax! What, you need some dick or something?" Her and Trina, who had no idea that the joke was on her, fell out laughing.

"Nah, I don't need no dick. I'm sure you done had enough dick in you for the both of us." I knew that was a low blow, but she asked for it. More and more, she was starting to look more like an enemy than a friend.

"Girl, please! What was that supposed to do? Hurt my feelings?"

"Nope. Not at all. I'm sure you know this about yourself already."

"Really? Oh, okay. Well, I see you're in a bad mood right now, so I'ma let you go. I'll call you later or something." She hung up without even letting me respond. I looked at the phone in disbelief and shook my head. Either it was the guilt that made her hang up so quickly, or she couldn't handle the truth. Either way, I knew that I needed to reconsider our friendship. There had been too many red flags in the past year when it came to her. From Kareem to what happened when she visited me to what she was doing right now. It all screamed untrustworthy and because of that, I couldn't help but think that if she could do it to Trina, she could and would probably do it to me, if she hadn't already. Like my mother always said, a leopard doesn't change its spots.

Chapter 27

The argument with Rich's bitch ass had my adrenaline pumping. Now I was really ready to get my hands dirty on some savage shit. My whole life I felt like people always went out of their way to doubt me, but not this time. This time, I was going to make shit happen. I swerved through traffic down Memorial Highway, looking out for the first check-cashing place that I could find. It was Friday and it was a few days short of the first of the month, so I knew it would be packed. But in order to put my plan into place, I had to cash my check first. After standing in line for what seemed like forever, I finally got my check cashed. Now it was time for a wardrobe change.

When I pulled up to my apartment, I immediately noticed Tony standing on my porch, smoking a blunt. *What the fuck does this nigga want,* I thought to myself. I was tempted to drive off before he noticed me, but my curiosity got the best of me. I threw my car in park and got out. Instead of going up on my porch where he was standing, I leaned against my car with my arms folded. The distance between us would keep him from trying anything stupid.

"Can I help you?" I asked with mad attitude. He smirked while taking a pull from his blunt.

"You know I always liked how feisty you are, ma. What you doing with a square ass nigga like Q?" I rolled my eyes. I was not about to entertain this nigga. He had already wasted enough of my time and energy the last time we interacted.

"OK, so I see that I can't help you. In that case, you need to get off my porch, please and thank you." He looked amused.

"Actually, you can help me, ma. In more ways than you know. But for now, I just came by to see wassup with Q. He's supposed to be making a major move for me this weekend;

something that can't be put off or rescheduled. I need that to happen." I laughed out loud. This dude was something else.

"Let me get this straight. You want Q to come home so he can make some bogus ass move for you, yet you ain't mentioned shit about helping to get him out? You're funnier than I thought, you know that? Now please get off my porch with your nonsense. Thank you." He clenched his jaw.

"This shit ain't no game, V." I laughed some more.

"Oh, trust me, I know it ain't no game. I'm the motherfucker that's been out her making shit happen, remember? Because of me and ONLY me, Q will be home tonight. Once he is, y'all can discuss this so-called major move. But if I'm lucky, this time away might've given him some time to realize just how much of a snake you are and then y'all won't be discussing shit." He smiled. I mugged him.

"Aight. Bet. Let me know when you ready to fuck with a real nigga, ma."

He walked off my porch and headed in the direction of the trap. *Let me hurry up and get Q's ass out before this nigga tries some stupid shit,* I thought to myself. Once he was out of sight, I ran into my crib and started changing my clothes. I grabbed my good bra that pushed my little boobies up and gave me pretend cleavage and paired it with a cropped top that showed off my flat stomach and diamond belly ring. I grabbed a black pair of leggings that were somewhat see-through and made my booty look scrumptious. Last but not least, I threw on my most comfortable pair of Air Maxes. I glossed my lips, put on my bamboo earrings, and let my hair loose from the bun it was in. I looked in the mirror and smiled. *Yeaaah, this will do!* I looked at the time on my cell phone; it was already noon. I needed to get this shit over and done with. I went outside and hopped back in my car. This time, I was heading towards the gas station near Aaliyah's school.

The moment I pulled into the station, I could feel the butterflies building up in my stomach. This plan was either going to help me get Q out of jail today or send my ass to jail right with him. Either way, it was too late to turn back now. I took a hundred-dollar bill and a fifty-dollar bill out of my wallet. Then I took four hundred dollar bills and one fifty-dollar bill out of the package of the realistic play money that I bought at the joke shop. I nervously placed the real money on top of the fake money and got ready to go inside.

As I reached for my car door handle, my phone started ringing, damn near making me jump out of my own skin. *Okay, Victoria, you gotta relax. It's just your damn cell phone ringing.* I tried calming myself down. I looked at the screen. It was my mother calling.

"Hey, Ma, wassup?"

"Don't hey, Ma, wassup me, girl! What happened to calling me back yesterday? Shit, I would've even taken a call back today."

"I'm sorry, mommy. I honestly forgot. I've just been so busy," I lied.

"Umm-hmm. Too busy for your own damn momma. What a shame." I could tell she was about to get started, so I tried to end the conversation before she did.

"Ma, it's not even like that, I promise. Can I call you back, though? I'm kinda in the middle of something."

"You're always in the middle of something, let you tell it. I'm starting to worry. Is everything okay, Victoria?"

"Yes, Ma, everything is fine." I tried not to sound annoyed, but it didn't work.

"Okay. Well, just know that you don't ever have to hesitate to ask for my help with anything. Whatever it is, Victoria. We may not always see eye to eye on things, but I am your mother until death do us part, which means I will always look out for you. You understand me?" Her words were so sincere that I was tempted to come right out and ask for the $500, but my pride wouldn't let me.

"I know, Ma. I love you. I'll call you later." I hung up before things could get any more emotional. This was not what I needed right now. Something inside of me told me to say a quick prayer for what I was about to do. I know that seems a little hypocritical, but I followed my gut and did it anyways.

"Father God, please forgive me for the sin that I am about to commit. I know that my actions have not been pleasing to You, but I ask that You see past my actions and know my heart. Father, please watch over Aaliyah, my mom, and Q if I get caught after I embark on this journey in the name of love. Although I know You do not agree with what I am about to do, please protect me and hold me in the palms of Your hand. In Jesus' name, I pray, Amen."

Instantly, tears began to roll down my face. I didn't know if it was fear or guilt about what I was about to do, but I couldn't stop them. I took a deep breath and shook off the tears I felt building up and put my game face back on. I told myself scared money don't make no money and stepped out of my car. I walked into the gas station and my favorite Indian friend was at the register, just like I knew he would be. *Word, this is about to be easy peasy,* I thought to myself. As soon as he noticed me walk in, he started flirting, just like any other time.

"Ohhh, it is my favorite pretty lady! Looking more pretty than usual today." I assumed that compliment had everything to do with my see-through leggings, lack of underwear and exposed cleavage and stomach. But fuck it, whatever caught his attention.

"Hey, you," I flirted back while walking around the store like I was looking for something. "How you doing today?" I made sure to put an extra switch in my hips so my booty jiggled when I was walking by the counter. I walked over to the freezer and bent over to grab a can of soda off the bottom shelf. I knew he was staring at my ass because he never even bothered to answer my question. After I had grabbed the soda, I turned to walk back towards the counter. I wanted to die laughing at how he was trying to ring people up and stare at me at the same time. I watched as a customer told him ten dollars on pump 4. He stuck the money in the register and put the amount in the computer without ever taking his eyes off me for more than three seconds. *Perfect.*

I walked up to the counter and purposely leaned in a little so he could stare at my pushed up boobs. His eyes widened and I struggled not to laugh.

"Let me get this soda and a $600 money order, boo."

The fact that I was asking for a $600 money order wasn't anything out of the ordinary. I always went there to get my money order for my rent because he never charged me the money order fee. Q and I would always make jokes about how he was always staring so damn hard that I could give him paper instead of money and he wouldn't know the difference. Today, I was going to test that theory out.

I pulled a single dollar bill out from one pocket of my cropped jean jacket and then grabbed the fake money mixed with real money out of my other pocket. I put it all together and handed it to him with confidence. I even gave him a little wink and just as I expected, he opened the register and stuck the money in without even looking. He was damn near drooling and I was damn near shaking with fear. I secretly let out a huge sigh of relief as I watched him close the register drawer and proceed to make my money order, still never taking his eyes off me. When he handed me the money order, I made sure to rub his hand a little to put the icing on the cake.

"Byyyyeeee," I said as I strutted out of the door.

Oh my fucking God, this shit really worked, I screamed on the inside. I guess God did hear my prayers. I was so excited I wanted to jump up and down, but I had to keep it cool. I knew I wasn't in the clear until I pulled out of the parking lot. I was about one hundred feet away from my car when I heard someone yelling.

"Hey! Hey, you! Wait a minute!" I could tell by the accent that it was the Indian guy from the register, but I acted like I didn't hear him and kept walking. This time, I walked a little faster. He would have to catch me. I wasn't going down easy.

"Wait a minute! Stop right there! I am talking to you!"

This time, he yelled a little louder, which had me ready to shit bricks. I thought about running and jumping into my car before he could catch up to me. Right before I made a dash to my car, I felt a hand grip my shoulder tightly.

To Be Continued...